Augustin Daly, Alexandre Dumas

Monsieur Alphonse

a play in three acts - Volume 1

Augustin Daly, Alexandre Dumas

Monsieur Alphonse
a play in three acts - Volume 1

ISBN/EAN: 9783337090081

Printed in Europe, USA, Canada, Australia, Japan

Cover: Foto ©Andreas Hilbeck / pixelio.de

More available books at **www.hansebooks.com**

MONSIEUR ALPHONSE

A Play in Three Acts.

By ALEXANDER DUMAS, Fils.

ADAPTED AND AUGMENTED

BY

AUGUSTIN DALY.

AS ACTED AT THE FIFTH AVENUE THEATRE, FOR THE
FIRST TIME, APRIL 25th, 1874.

NEW YORK:
PRINTED, AS MANUSCRIPT ONLY, FOR THE AUTHOR.
1886.

DRAMATIS PERSONÆ AND ORIGINAL CAST.

CAPTAIN MONTAGLIN, one Man in Ten Thousand,
$\qquad$ MR. CHARLES FISHER

MONSIEUR OCTAVE, one Man of Many . . . MR. GEORGE CLARKE

JOVIN, on the trail of Monsieur Alphonse . . . . . MR. JAMES LEWIS

REMY, an old hulk, laid up for coast duty . MR. FRANK HARDENBERG

RAYMONDE, an old man's Darling and a young man's Slave,
$\qquad$ MISS ADA DYAS

MADAME GUICHARD, "Born So" . . . . MISS FANNY DAVENPORT

MANON, a peasant . . . . MRS. G. H. GILBERT

BONETTE, her daughter . . . . MISS NINA VARIAN

ADRIENNE, one of the Nameless . . . . BIJOU HERON

ACT I.—Noon! Monsieur Alphonse abducts the little savage, and Captain Montaglin gives her a home.

ACT II.—Afternoon! THREE CONTESTS!

ACT III.—Evening! Madame Guichard places herself on the public records, and is deceived for the last time by M. Alphonse!

ACT I.

SCENE.—*The interior of a country house near the sea. Beyond is a garden and a conservatory, the entrance to which is at* C. *by a flight of steps. To the* R. *is a library, to the* L. *is the door of entrance.*

The curtain rises to the music of an old sea song. REMY *enters with a naval coat, which he is brushing. Advances down stairs from conservatory, singing.*

> "Oh, oh, my messmates now we'll sing
> The glories of Neptune, the ocean king,
> And the fun that's had on the O—O—shun!"

Remy. [*Admiring the coat.*] Laid up on the stocks a whole year, and just as trim as ever! [*Brushes.*] Clean as a holy-stoned deck arter a dryin' sun. Ah! How often I've seed this coat marchin' back'ard and for'ard on the quarter, an' him as was inside it—brave and cool when every other mother's son of us was up to the taffrails in fear o' the comin' squall. And so he's off agin to-morrow! [*Folds coat at* L. *table.*] And I ain't! The first voyage old Remy has let him go alone!—and that's what I got to thank the rheumatix for! Ah! [*Shakes his head, and brushes off a speck from the folded coat.*]

MANON *and* BONETTE *enter up the steps at back; they peer curiously in.*

Hello! Who's them? Strange craft; not in our service! [*They huddle closely together, whispering; then look at Rem. and curtsey.*] Well! What's in the wind, folks? [BON. *pushes her mother to speak.*]
  Bonette. [R., *both curtseying.*] We must be in the right place! Speak to him, mother!
  Manon. [*Timid and simple.*] Please sir, who are you?
  Rem. [L., *imitating curtsey.*] Who am I? That's not bad from a boarding party dropping on your own deck! Who am I? I think I might ax who are you?
  Bon. Of course you might, sir—truly. We mean no offence, sir—truly.

Man. Certainly, the old gentleman ought to know who we are. This is my daughter, Bonette, sir! [*They curtsey; she puts* BON. C.]

Bon. And this is my mother, sir, Manon! [*They curtsey; she puts* MAN. C.]

Rem. You don't say so! Now I knows a good deal. But I never saw you in the village.

Man. No, sir! We came a long way.

Bon. Yes, sir—truly.

Rem. [L.] And what do you want?

Man. [C., *hesitating cough;* BON. *coughs in response.*] First, sir—you remember we asked you who you were?

Bon. Yes, sir, we must know first to whom we speak, sir—truly.

Man. It's only fair as we told you our names—

Rem. [*Folding coat on chair, at* L. *table.*] To hear mine, eh! Well—I'm Remy.

Man. and Bon. Remy! [MAN. *puts on specs. They draw aside and look at a paper, which* MAN. *carries in her hand; appear much puzzled, and they shake their heads.*]

Rem. [*Singing to himself.*]

> "There once was a sailor
> And he did have a wife,
> And she did love the sailor
> As she did love her life."

Man. Shall I show him the paper?

Bon. Let's be certain first. Ask him if he's the master of the house.

Man. [*Pushing* Bon. *to* C.] That's so. You ask him.

Bon. [C.] Please sir—tell me first—is this your house— truly?

Rem. Would you ax a bos'n leaning on the gunnel of a seventy-four if that wor his craft? No, no, my dolly! [*Chucks* BON. *under the chin. She is offended and starts away to* R. H.] I'm only shipped—not in commission. The Captain is out in the orchard yonder with my lady. I'm but a servant.

Man. [*Re-assured.*] A servant. [*To* Bon.] We can ask him.

Bon. Yes.

Man. [C.] Will you look at this paper, please, and tell us if the lady lives here.

Rem. A lady? [*He looks over the paper she holds—not able to read.*] Is that the name of a lady? Well, you see, my eyes ain't what they used to be—they ain't. [*Aside.*] I'd wonder if they was, if I could read writing. [*Aloud.*] What does it say on it?

Man. Please, sir, we don't know. We can't read, sir.

Rem. Can't read! Poor critters! What, not that little bit? [*Takes the paper.*] There's not much of it. [*Hands it back.*] I am ashamed of you. Go out and find somebody to tell you what it means.

Man. Oh, I dare not, sir.

Rem. Dare not! Why not?

Man. We mustn't show it to a soul, except in the house—if this be the house.

Rem. What house?

Man. Where the lady lives.

Rem. What lady?

Bon. [*Very forward and pert.*] The lady with the sweet face who always used to come—!

Man. [*Stopping her.*] Take care, Bonette; take care. You know we promised not to betray the lady.

Rem. If you mean the Cap'n's lady—and mayhap you do, for she has the sweetest face I ever seed—even in my dreams o' night—why look you've only to wait here a bit, and you'll see her. Don't you know her name?

Man. No—for she wrote on this paper a long, long time ago—and only in case of great need we were to come here and show it in the house.

Rem. How did you know the house?

Man. She told us the road, and the name of the village, and that we should see the little ship—

Rem. [L.] A top o' the vane!! Well, now surely that was a good direction. The little ship! My eyes! You're right—it's the only ship in these parts. [*Gets to* L. *corner of steps and points down into garden.* MAN. *crosses to his* L. *and looks over his shoulder.*] It must be my lady. It's like her sensible way. Look here—there out in the orchard yonder—there now, walking with her husband!

Man. and Bon. [*Aside, nearing each other nervously.*] Her husband! [*Both getting to* R. H. *corner.*]

Man. [*To Rem.*] She has a husband?

Rem. Of course she has—and now he's coming this way.

Man. [*Nervous.*] Let's go, Bonette! We can come back! [*Draws her towards door,* L., *as if frightened.*]

Rem. Lay to! Where are you going? Why, my master is the kindest—Why what are you skeered of?

Man. [*To Rem.*] We will wait outside—and when the lady is alone—

Bon. [L.] We will come in.

Man. [C.] And please don't say anything to the master, sir—

Bon. Yes, truly, sir—please don't.

Rem. No! Well, I won't. Stand in the offing, and when you see the Cap'n go up to his room—sail in—there's your chance.

Man. Thank you, sir. Come, Bouette! Quick! I'm frightened already. [*Exeunt,* L.]

Rem. [*Looking after them.*] Lord, how timmersome some women-folks be! That is when they're poor and pretty. But when they are rich and ugly—Lord how brassy! They'd outface old Nick himself. Skeered o' the Cap'n! Lord! Lord! There he comes! Happy, as a boy, in his young wife—and she a hanging on his arm, and reaching up to his heart like the flowers that climb up our house and rest on its sunny, weather-beaten side.

MUSIC *of an old sea song, as* MONTAGLIN *enters gaily. He stops at the head of the steps, and calls.*

Montaglin. Come, Raymonde!

RAYMONDE *runs up the steps,* C., *and stops to fasten a flower in his buttonhole, at head of stairs.*

Raymonde. [R.] There!

Mon. I do believe, my girl, you forget that I'm not a young man, and that flowers have ceased to look well in my buttonhole for many a year.

Ray. Hush! I won't hear you say you are not a young man. [REM. *goes to* C., *looking down steps.*]

Mon. [L.] And I twenty years older than you.

Ray. A sailor never grows old. He takes to the sea when a boy, and is ever as young as the waves that are born anew every minute at his feet. He never gets to be a man except to command, to be obeyed and to be loved. [*Embraces her.*]

Mon. Happy boy and glad man when he has a wife like mine. But boy as he is, folks sometimes whisper—what a big daughter you have! Then I'm reminded of the great difference in our years. What a lovely little widow you would make!

Ray. Sir!

Mon. Here am I going to sea for a whole year! Sailors' wives always have the weeds before their eyes—seaweed and widow's weeds. When the husband goes into one, the wife—·

Ray. Ah!—the day before your departure to talk to me like that. Six years we have been married. You have been absent three. Three times I have beheld your face fading in the mist of that dreadful void—the sea! How I hate it—that vast and selfish sea! [*Crosses to* C.]

Mon. Hush! Or Remy will think that you are not fit to be a sailor's wife. [REM. *advances.*]

Ray. And Remy is worse than you. His eye brightens every time he prepares you for a voyage.

Rem. [L.] Beg pardon, me lady, but it makes me sad too, along o' this, that I can't go with him. But I know, Cap'n, I know, when an old hulk gets the dry rot in her, she must be laid up for a guardship in some muddy harbor. And when an old salt gets the rheumatix! Ah!

Ray. [C.] But you're to stay home and take care of me, Remy. Are you not proud of that duty? [*Putting her hat on table.*]

Rem. Aye, aye, my lady, some of us must be coast guard, and the honor's the same. [*Takes up coat—going, crosses to* C.] Beg your honor's pardon, but we couldn't send the coach to the station, the horses had gone to be shod when I got your honor's orders.

Mon. Carriage to the station? Oh! Ah! Well, never mind. He can walk.

Ray. You expect some one by the train?

Mon. Did I not tell you? Sure enough! We are to have a visitor. Ah! Remy—send down a saddle-horse for Monsieur Octave. [*Crosses to* C.]

Ray. [*Aside, and getting to table,* R. H.] Monsieur Octave!

Rem. Aye, aye, sir. Natalie can go. [*Exits,* L.]

Mon. You remember Octave? [*Sitting next to her at* R. H. *table.*]

Ray. [*Suppressing emotion.*] He called here once.

Mon. Yes, once, and only once. Two years ago. A precious young scamp. I recollect how you disliked him from the first, and he didn't stay long. Well, he has written me to say he intended to make me a visit on the eve of my departure, and wishes to see me on particular business.

Ray. [*Seated.*] Have you ever had any business with him?

Mon. Never. His business, whatever it is, evidently concerns himself and not me.

Ray. How do you know that?

Mon. Because he adds at the bottom of his letter, I have a great favor to ask of you.

Ray. Money, perhaps?

Mon. Perhaps! For I hear he is going to be married.

Ray. [*Relieved.*] No doubt. [*Crosses to* C.]

Mon. [*Rises.*] And time he was married. He has been a wild fellow. Here am I, the oldest friend of his family, I have been married six years, and during all that time he has been to visit us but once. [*Looks at watch.*] The train must be in now. Let me finish my letters before he arrives. There—don't frown too hard on the rascal when he comes—much as his bad reputation deserves every good woman's contempt. He is going to be married, and that is some attempt at reformation. [*Laughs, and exits,* R.]

MANON *and* BONETTE *peep in, as if watching* MON. *off.*

Ray. Octave here to-day! To ask a favor! What favor does he want of my husband? He whom I have seen but once in all these years!

MANON *and* BONETTE *steal in cautiously,* L.

Manon. Madame!
Ray. Who is there? [*Starts.*] You!!
Man. Madame knows we would not have intruded if—
Ray. [*Apprehensive, looks uneasily round the room and down the steps.*] Did any one see you enter?
Man. We spoke to the servant—an old man—
Ray. [*Still anxious.*] No one else?
Bonette. No one, madame—truly.
Ray. [*Relieved.*] That is right. And my name—you have not mentioned it in the village or on the road—
Man. Ah! no! We were too sly for that, madame! Bonette will tell you. [*Pushes her forward.*]
Bon. We gave no name, madame, and we did not show the little paper until we got here [*gesture of Ray.*]—to the old sailor. [*Crosses to* L., *as if to* Rem.]
Ray. And he cannot read. You have done well. Come to the point at once, then. Why have you sought me? Did you not receive the last sum of money I sent you?
Bon. Oh, yes, madame! It came on the very quarter day—like all the rest.
Ray. What then has happened?
Man. [*Tearfully, impressively.*] Madame, the child has been taken away.
Ray. [*Terrified whisper.*] Hush! hush! The child taken!
Man. [C.] Madame knows what care we have taken of her since eight years ago madame brought her—a little infant—to our poor cottage—
Ray. For heaven's sake, proceed! Adrienne has been taken away! Stolen from you? [*Getting away to* R.]
Man. Stolen? No, madame. I would have defended her

against a thief with every drop that lingers in my old body. She
was taken, madame, by one who claims the right.

Ray. [*Approaching her.*] You say—

Man. That gentleman who has been four or five times to
visit us.

Ray. [*Close to her.*] He—he came and took her away?

Man. Yes—Monsieur Alphonse!

Ray. When was this?

Man. Yesterday. We have not lost a moment in coming
here to tell you.

Ray. [*Nervous anger.*] And you let him take her! Him
that was a stranger!

Man. [*Timidly.*] Madame told us eight years ago—when he
came first—that he must be allowed to take the child out for a
walk, if he wished to. This time he came when my husband and
I were away. Bonette was there alone; she will tell you.
[*Crowding Bon. to* C.]

Bon. Yes, truly, I will. Monsieur Alphonse came and said
he wanted to take Adrienne to her home. I asked him: "Is it
to her mother you will take her?" He said: "Yes!" I said:
"To the lady's?" meaning you, madame. [RAY. *is affected.*]
He said: "Oh no; that is a kind friend, but not her mother!"
Then I said: "But, monsieur, the lady is the only one that ever
visits little Adrienne—*she* comes nearly every month, while you
come so seldom. We ought to tell the lady!" He answered:
"Certainly, tell her at once!" All this sounded so fair, madame,
that I let Adrienne go with him. We cried together at parting,
madame, truly, we did—for I loved her, and she always slept
with me and in my arms. [*Gets to* L., *weeping loudly. Both cry.*]

Man. My husband is furious, madame. You should have
heard him. He couldn't have taken it more to heart, if Adrienne
had been his own flesh and blood!" "There," he said; five
hundred francs a year gone!" I was terribly frightened, because I thought of you, and that for the first time we must seek
you out, and bring you bad news. But Bonette said to me:
"After all, as the lady is not Adrienne's mother!"—

Bon. [*Crying.*] For you know, madame, thoughts will come
into one's head—although you never whispered a word to us in
confidence, we thought the child was yours.

Man. Yes, madame, for you know you let it call you
mamma—

Ray. [*Much agitated, looking round the room, passes to back
of table so as to meet them, as she says "hush."*] Hush! I do
not blame you. You could do nothing but obey the wishes of
this—

Man. Monsieur Alphonse! Yes, madame, and he was always a very civil spoken gentleman. And—

Ray. [*Takes portemonnaie from table, R., and cutting her short.*] Here is money for you. Say no word of me or of the child again—to any one. Let us both be as if dead. Your husband's silence shall be bought as well.

Man. [*Pleased at getting the money.*] Oh, madame! Don't mind him. Angry, but soon over it.

Bon. Father will be melted when we tell him you forgive us. [*Shaking her mother's hand with the money in it.*]

Ray. Do not speak of me. Say only this—money will soon be sent him. Go! I hear a footstep. I thank you for your kindness. Go!

Man. Ah! Madame, I am sorry we had to bring you bad tidings. Had I been there the child would not—[*Pushing Bon.*] But this fool of a girl! It would serve you right, hussy, if the lady scolded you well. Go home!

Bon. [*Whimpering.*] I couldn't help it, truly. [*Exit, pushed off by* MAN. *She cries till out of hearing.*]

As they go off at L., JOVIN *suddenly appears at* C., *looks after them, and then dodges back.*

Ray. [R. C.] The child taken away yesterday! To be restored, he said, to it's own home! How can I find the solution of this enigma? That letter of Octave and the favor he seeks! At all hazards I must hear every word that passes between him and my husband. What misfortune is about to overtake me? Or, rather, what new punishment hangs over my head. In a few minutes he will be here. From the conservatory I can watch his coming—and from the library I can overhear all. [*At door of room, R.*] To watch! To watch! [*Goes out.*]

JOVIN *emerges, and looks after her.*

Jovin. Whew! Such a race as I had to get here before him. He's at the station—waiting for a carriage to be sent for Monsieur Octave from Captain Montaglin's. So while he stamped about at the depot, I steamed away for the house of Captain Montaglin, to pick up information as instructed. That sorrel mare I passed on the way must have been going for him. Bless my lucky stars! I always thought I was better than a horse and buggy— and the dog under it. Who appears for examination? [*Looks about him.*] Oh, for a simple domestic! Even the old salt I saw piloting those women down to the gate! Well, all I have to do, is to wait for kind fortune to put into the witness-box some person or persons—male, female, or otherwise, whom I can interrogate in the cause of my interesting client.

REMY *enters,* L.

Ah! Here's my tarry toplight friend!]

Remy. [L., *pauses, taking quid. Stares at him, and then looks round.*] How did you manage to pass my guns?

Jov. Eh! [*Looks about him, as if for the guns.*]

Rem. Drop alongside and report.

Jov. [*Aside.*] I was not mistaken. He is a mariner. [*Aloud.*] You are one of the domestics, I suppose?

Rem. Domestics? Well, I'm first mate below stairs—if that's what you mean.

Jov. And your master?

Rem. The Cap'n?—

Jov. Captain? [*Looks in his note book.*] Yes, Captain Montaglin. Name all right.

Rem. Have you got the skipper's name in the log?

Jov. In the log?

Rem. In the writin' book there.

Jov. Oh! I see! Yes! I wish I knew a few nautical terms to converse with you comfortably, my friend.

Rem. Lord, it would improve you! Indeed it would. But, I say—report yourself—what craft are you and where bound?

Jov. Craft? Eh? Oh! I see! You mean me. Oh! I'm on particular business—I suppose I'm what he'd call a rakish little cutter.

Rem. Humph! And if I may be so bold—whom do you want to see?

Jov. Anybody that can give me the information I'm after. You see—to express it in your own terse vocabulary—I'm not bound for any particular port. I'm a cruiser.

Rem. A cruiser? Then sheer off—till I know your flag and your commission. Where's your papers?

Jov. My papers are at present the slight volume you are pleased to call my log. My commission is from that government of which we are all faithful subjects—ahem, the petticoat! And my flag, necessarily to carry out the simile, is a piece of dimity. In other words, to translate from your language into mine: I'm on a tour of inquiry, for a female client. Fair woman is the motive, my venerable barnacle.

Rem. Well, that's harmless anyhow.

Jov. [*Opens book.*] And as a mariner, who, I take it, has often sailed under the flag, [REM. *chuckles*] I count on you for information. This Captain Montaglin—follows the sea, eh?—retired or active?

Rem. Retired! Not a bit of it. He goes off to-morrow.

Jov. Married or single?

Rem. Married, in course! Else what would he be doing with a house ashore?

Jov. His wife goes with him, eh? No! Ah! Stays at home?

Rem. At home, and I'm to keep watch, and watch over her.

Jov. [*Stage, R., writing in his book.*] Extraordinary! Husband goes away. Wife has to be watched.

Rem. I said watched.

Jov. Well, I said watched.

Rem. Oh! I thought you said washed.

Jov. They keep a deal of company, I suppose?

Rem. [L.] Well, some craft is allus in the offing.

Jov. Ah! Visitors from Paris sometimes, I suppose?

Rem. Well, you suppose wrong then. I can't say as I ever see any pleasure craft about here.

Jov. While I was at the station I heard a gentleman inquiring about the Captain.

Rem. Oh, that was likely Monsieur Octave; an old friend—

Jov. Of madame?

Rem. No, of the Captain. I've knowed him for years myself.

Jov. He comes here often?

Rem. [R.] Well—not often.

Jov. What do you call not often?

Rem. Well, I should call every day *very often*.

Jov. Yes. So should I.

Rem. [L.] And I should call once a week *quite often*.

Jov. My views exactly.

Rem. And I should call once a month *often*.

Jov. Oh get on; crowd on more sail.

Rem. And lastly I guess you'd call once a year *not* often.

Jov. [*Ready with pencil to note down.*] I would. So he comes once a year?

Rem. Well, no he don't! He's only been here once in six years—that is only once since the Cap'n and my lady was married.

Jov. Rather odd for an old friend, eh?

Rem. Yes, it is. For the Captain and his father was boys. I've been to their home years ago, with my master; I carried his portemanteau. We used to go nearly every week.

Jov. Every week! Ah! That's what you'd call *quite often*, eh?

Rem. Yaas! an' I seed him there—a little fellow. And now you knows as much as I does.

Jov. Thank you, my friend. I'm very much obliged. And now, can I do anything for you in return for your politeness?

Rem. You hain't got a bit of 'baccy about you?

Jov. I regret to say that as I do not indulge in the solace, I must reply in the negative.

Rem. I axed you if you had any 'baccy about you?

Jov. And I was forced to return a negative and unsatisfactory response! [*Puts up his book.*]

Rem. [*Aside, and scratching his head.*] Dash my lights, if I think he knows what 'baccy is, and is hiding his ignorance in Greek. [*Aloud.*] Ah! There's Natalie's hoofs on the road. Monsieur Octave is come. Wait here and you'll see him. [*Going* c.] My eye! Not to know what 'baccy is. [*Exits down steps.*]

Jov. He's here. Wait and see him? Oh, no! But keep him in sight?—oh yes! I wonder if I could! [*Looks around.*] There's a room! [*Goes* R., *looks in and starts back.*] A lady in there! Coming in from the garden, and in a hurry. No go! I had better continue to get out and go back to the telegraph office. It's about time to send another message. [*Writes at* L. *table.*] "Tracked him here; Captain Montaglin's; old friend of family; married." That will do. Ten sous ten words—and repeat for accuracy. [*Looks off* c.] He comes. I go! [*Exits,* L.]

REMY *enters,* c., *showing in* OCTAVE.

Remy. [R.] I'll run up and tell the Captain.

Octave. Do, my good fellow. [*Gives him a coin.*] You havn't forgotten me, I find.

Rem. No, your honor. Ah, here he is!

MONTAGLIN *enters,* R.; REM. *goes out* L.

Montaglin. [R.] So you've come again, eh? You precious young rascal! It's so long since I saw you that I thought you were dead and buried.

Oct. My dear Captain, I knew you were going away to-morrow, and as I had not seen you for two years, I wanted to present my respects before your departure. Madame is well?

Mon. [R.] Very.

Oct. I have a great many things to say to you.

Mon. I supposed so from the tone of your letter.

Oct. Mysterious, was it not? But I could not trust all to paper.

Mon. Why not?

Oct. Because I have a great favor to ask of you. A favor I could ask of no one but my father, and as he is not living—of the man who promised him to be a father to me.

Mon. That was on condition that you chose to be a son to me. You have chosen to be a stranger.

Oct. Oh, sir! I do not rely on my own deserts. I rely on your good heart.

Mon. You are right. I should hear you, without discouraging you in advance. It is the first favor you have ever asked of me. Go on!

Oct. You know, sir, that I am about to get married?

Mon. [*Coolly.*] I heard so.

Oct. [L.] Captain! Once, several years ago, I was known to be perhaps a little wild—news of it may have reached you.

Mon. News of it did reach me.

Oct. Well, sir—but whether you grant me the favor I ask or not, this must be absolutely confidential—I rely on your discretion—I, I have a daughter—a little girl—

Mon. You? A—[*Motions with his hand, as to a little child.*]

Oct. [*Same action, but left hand higher, as if indicating a taller child.*] Yes.

Mon. [*Linking his arm in Oct.'s in a friendly manner.*] Oh, I understand. You are about to get married to the mother of this child?

Oct. No.

Mon. No?

Oct. My intended wife does not know of the existence of this child.

Mon. [*Recoiling.*] Oh!

Oct. And she must never know. She would never forgive me.

Mon. Why?

Oct. Because she believes I never loved any one but her.

Mon. [R.] Poor woman!

Oct. You pity her because I keep her in ignorance? It is for her happiness I do so.

Mon. Bah!

Oct. You have a bad opinion of me.

Mon. Very.

Oct. Why?

Mon. Because I have always a poor opinion of the frivolous and vain.

Oct. Frivolous! Perhaps. But vain—no! And you will soon see that my frivolity is only assumed. One must howl with the wolves, and in a world which sneers at virtue and calls it hypocrisy, I must sneer with the others or be eaten by the ravenous pack!

Mon. Well, to your story. [*Both sit.*]

Oct. [L.] Well then—I have a daughter almost ten years of age.

Mon. Ten?

Oct. Yes.

Mon. Well, you have not lost any time. And where is she?

Oct. Brought up by a family of peasants in the country.

Mon. And her mother?

Oct. Her mother does not know her now.

Mon. What has become of this amiable mother?

Oct. Married and left France. [*Rises to evade* MON.'s *searching glance.*]

Mon. What heartlessness! Why are you now about to marry?

Oct. Don't you approve of my marrying and settling down? [*Reseats himself.*]

Mon. Under the circumstances, no.

Oct. You wouldn't say so if you saw my wife.

Mon. Your intended wife! Well! I don't know her—perhaps I shall never know her. But I hear she is a woman wholly without education or refinement.

Oct. Not refined, certainly—but clever.

Mon. And rich! And if she were not rich, you would not think of her. [*Rise.*] Now here is what I condemn. You are in the very flower of manhood. You are at an age when a man can prove all his energy, his dignity and his generosity. With some work you can rise to a great position. You might live for this child. You might give her all the love, the duty, the devotion, that should have been given to her mother. Instead of being the loser on all sides, she might have gained a double share of happiness. But what do you do? You put her out of sight, in order to marry a woman for her money. You are wrong— and I can tell you so, because your father, [*sits beside Octave*] brave sailor that he was, died in my arms, my best, my earliest friend; because your poor mother soon followed him; because the last sou of their fortune has been dissipated in your follies; and because you have had no one to guide, to counsel, or to warn you—and because I owe it to the memory of your father to do so when I can.

Oct. [*Gushingly taking his hand.*] I thank you, sir! But think—what better guide can I have than a good wife—

Mon. A good wife! She! [*Rising.*] Ah well!

2

Oct. Oh, then, since you will not listen to me—[*Taking his hat, putting his chair by table,* L. H.]

Mon. You are going?

Oct. Yes.

Mon. Sit down. [*Pressing him back into seat.*] If I have spoken harshly it is not because I take advantage of the moment you ask a favor of me, but only because I hoped to see in you—

Oct. What?

Mon. One spark of love for this poor child. One sign of paternal feeling.

Oct. Love for her! Captain, you do not know all. From her birth I have reared this child, kept her, schooled her, trained her. All this for ten years, when I might have abandoned her, as so many have been abandoned. Would I have done this, if I had no love for her? [*Mock tears.*]

Mon. [*Cordially.*] Give me your hand. From this moment I begin to look upon you as an honest man. Tell me, what is it you wish? [*Sitting next to him.*]

Oct. [*Confidentially, and assuming a friendly manner.*] This. My intended wife—Madame Guichard—

Mon. Is that her name? Madame Guichard! Well?

Oct. She will never consent to receive this child. I am compelled to conceal even the existence of Adrienne from her; and at ten years a young girl must have a home—a guardian. Now here is my idea. You have no children—you leave to-morrow on a long voyage—your wife will be absolutely alone: will you let me bring Adrienne here to her—let me give her to your wife to keep—to rear—to take as her own? For never could a child have a better mother, if you can persuade Madame Montaglin to receive her.

Mon. [*Rising, pushes his chair to* C.] Bring your child whenever you will. I have but to ask my wife—she is too good and compassionate to refuse.

Oct. [*Rises.*] You are sure she will consent?

Mon. I am sure.

Oct. Then I will go and bring Adrienne here. I left her at the inn near the station.

Mon. And I will seek my wife at once. [*Taking his hat and calling as he goes out.*] Raymonde! Raymonde! [*Exits,* C. *steps.*]

Oct. [*Looking in triumph after Mon.*] Done! [*About to go,* L.]

RAYMONDE *enters,* R.

Raymonde. [R.] Stay!

Oct. You!

Ray. I have heard all. What infamy is this?

Oct. [*Advancing.*] Infamy? I thought you would be only too glad to have your child always near you.

Ray. [R.] But not at the cost of this deception on my husband. Why did you not warn me of this plot against a generous and unsuspecting man?

Oct. Because I knew you would not consent.

Ray. And you were right. You shall not move one step further in this baseness. [*Crosses to* L.]

Oct. [*Quickly.*] There is one other way left. Confess everything to your husband.

Ray. It is what I should have done before my marriage. But I had not the courage. I would die of the shame—and I thought it better to die of my grief. Oh, that I could! [*Sinking into seat,* L. H.]

Oct. Then I'm not to go for the child?

Ray. No.

Oct. Very well. It will not be my fault, if you see her no more. [*Going up, takes hat from* R. *table.*]

Ray. See her no more! What will you do?

Oct. [*Playing with back of chair.*] Well, she can't stay with those people forever, and I am about to get married. My intended is jealousy itself. Forever prying into my movements. Even to setting spies on me. If she discovers the child she will break off the marriage—and that will not do. If she discovers her after the marriage, I shall live in limbo for the rest of my existence. Besides, when she learns of the child, she won't stop there, she will begin to look for—hem, somebody else. And if she found out Adrienne's relation to you—she is capable of doing you all the harm she could.

Ray. Peace! Peace! I pray you!

Oct. [*Confidentially, as he sits beside her.*] Your husband goes away to-morrow. You will want to see Adrienne as usual: I don't wish it to continue, if she has no hope of ever sharing your home. But, if you loved her you would bless me for the suggestion I make. Now look at it. If she came to live with you, it would only be natural for her, in the course of time, to call you mamma—and nobody could think it strange. Chance has made you the wife of an old friend of my family—an old friend who knows me from infancy. Let us make use of this chance—chance is the providence of the bold.

Ray. [*Rises, hand on table.*] Oh! What kind of a man are you?

Oct. [*Rises.*] My dear—[*With affectionate familiarity.*]

Ray. Sir! [*Crosses to* R., *in disgust.*]

Oct. I beg pardon; I am too familiar. Well, my dear madame, I am a man who takes life as it is—but who will not be thwarted by people, nor by things. I have made up my mind to place Adrienne in this house. I am wrong to waste words with you. You must consent—because he has consented. [*Turns towards* C.]

Ray. Yes, he is incapable of suspecting evil in any one. [*Montaglin's voice heard outside.* "*Never mind, I will find her.*"]

Oct. I hear his voice. He has been seeking you.

Ray. His voice rouses me to my duty. I forbid this crime! Do you hear me? I forbid—

Oct. [*Stage,* L.] Too late! He is here.

MONTAGLIN *enters,* C.

Montaglin. [*Down* C., *cheerfully.*] Ah, my darling! I was hunting for you all over the garden. What, Octave, here yet! Look at him, my love! I have spoken harshly of him to you. Well, forget it all! He has a child! He loves her, and he is about to become a good and honest man. [*To Oct.*] Go, bring your daughter. And henceforth the little one shall have father and mother here.

Oct. I obey! [*Exits,* L., *with meaning look at Ray., who turns away and buries her face in her hands at table.*]

Mon. [*Approaching her.*] My darling.

Ray. [*In chair at table.*] Oh, how good you are!

Mon. Am I? Then kiss me.

Ray. [*Rises.*] Yes, indeed! [*Puts her arms around his neck.*] You do not know how much I love you.

Mon. Truly?

Ray. [R.] You doubt me? You are wrong. I have for you such respect—such pride—such reverence—

Mon. Ah, you say all the words in the world—but not one of them is love.

Ray. Such love!! So profound, so powerful, so new, and strange, that I think but of you, live but in your life—see in you only my dream of dreams. Do I not owe everything to you? Did you not find me a poor working girl—sewing day and night to earn my little crust of bread? Did you not give me your heart, your name—make me rich, happy, envied? Lift me to the height of your fame, make me a part of your glorious life? Before all this I knew nothing—saw nothing—was nothing. Now I live! I love! I bless you with every breath I breathe—and when my death can spare you a single sorrow, I will die with a smile of happiness, with a song of joy.

Mon. [*His arm round her waist, her hands on his shoulder. During speech he takes both hands warmly.*] I believe—and I love you! You remember when I asked you six years ago if you would be my wife, I told you that our marriage would perhaps not be such as the dreams of young girls picture; and we made our contract at the altar as man and woman joined in one against all the ills of life. You were so modest, so sad, so devoted to that poor old woman whose reason had left her, your sole and only relative; and I felt I had the right to offer you my name and my love to save you from the loneliness and the misery that would follow her death. I said to you—do you wish a friend— one who can be with you but two or three months each year, but who wishes to know in his long voyage, that there is some- where a heart that thinks of him and counts the days till his return. Will you be my companion for a few years, and my daughter for all the rest? And you accepted. But I demanded no more. I have the right to ask for no more. [RAY. *throws herself upon his breast.*]

Enter OCTAVE, C., *gaily, with* ADRIENNE *by the hand. She is dressed simply in white, like a little girl.*

Octave. Here's our little savage! [*Aside to Mon.*] She calls me Monsieur. She does not know that I am her father. Don't tell her.

Mon. [*Crosses to seat,* L.] Rest easy about that. [*To Ad., who has been looking at Ray. all the time.*] Come, my daughter. Every one in this house wishes to be kind to you. [*Sits, and has Ad. to stand before him.*] How old are you?

Adrienne. Ten. [*To Oct.*] Am I not, sir? [OCT. *nods.*]

Mon. And your name?

Ad. [L. C.] Adrienne! In the village every one called me Adrienne Freneau, because Freneau was the name of my foster- father and mother; but truly and indeed I have no other name but Adrienne. [MON. *looks at Oct.*]

Oct. [C.] Pretty name, isn't it?

Mon. [*To Ad.*] Then you have no relatives?

Ad. I never had any. I never saw anybody except Mon- sieur, [*indicates Oct.*] who knew my parents, and who promised them when they died to take care of me. He has been very good to me. [*Going to Oct.*] But to-day more than ever be- fore. [*She holds out her hand to Oct.*]

Mon. [*Energetically.*] Take her in your arms!

Oct. [*Complies superficially.*] She knows that I think a great deal of her.

Mon. [*To Ad.*] You expect to be very happy here?

Ad. I am sure of it.

Mon. Then you did not like it where you have lived. [*Arm around her waist again.*]

Ad. Oh, yes! But then they did not know me always—and I could not—I could not talk to them as I wished.

Mon. Ah! You wished somebody to talk to, eh?

Ad. Yes.

Mon. About what?

Ad. Oh, about so many things. For I have often strange thoughts that come to me, and I would so love to speak of my thoughts—and I will—to madame, if she will let me. [*Advances to Ray., who turns away to* R.] But don't be afraid, madame, I'm not a bad girl. I was very sick—here and here—[*places her hand on her throat and on her bosom*] and I cried so much—all alone—that I made myself worse. Oh, I cannot tell you how I suffered for want of some one to cry with, and to speak to, and to love. But now I am getting well again.

Mon. [L. C.] Why did you not speak to monsieur? [*Looking at Oct.*]

Ad. [*Getting back to Mon.*] He could not come to see me often, and when he came he was always so hurried.

Oct. [*Embarrassed, down* L.] I couldn't get leave of absence, you know, from my department.

Mon. [*To Oct.*] I understand. [*To Ad.*] I wager now, you know exactly how many times Monsieur has been to see you?

Ad. Oh yes! Six times.

Oct. [*In answer to Mon.'s look.*] Oh, I went oftener when she was a little girl. She can't remember.

Mon. Evidently. [*To Ad.*] Well, my dear little child, *I* cannot talk much with you now, because I have to go away to-morrow.

Ad. [*Affectionately.*] You are going away; and I just came.

Mon. But I will come back, and then we will talk, talk, talk! all about the things you have learned while I was away. But let me speak to you of one thing. Heaven!—you have heard them speak of heaven, my child?

Ad. Oh, yes, sir! But I think God has heard oftener of me, because I have prayed to him so much.

Mon. Well, my child, He who in His wisdom hath ordained that you should have neither father or mother on earth, has likewise ordained that we should have no little children.

Ad. [*Joyfully.*] I understand! You will be my father and mother, and I will be your child.

Mon. Would you like that?

Ad. Oh! yes indeed!

Mon. [*Rising and giving her his hand as to a great personage. Lifts child on the chair on which he had been sitting, and takes both her hands.*] Then it is agreed, signed, and sealed, between the high contracting parties! [*She takes both his hands in hers, and he kisses her on the forehead.*] And now I leave you with madame, who will duly instal you into our household, while I go to continue my work. Besides, two ladies who are to live together for the balance of their lives ought to have a great deal to say to each other. [*Lifting her down, and putting her across near Ray.*]

Ad. Oh, indeed, they must!

Mon. [*To Oct.*] You will dine with us?

Oct. [L.] No. I—

Mon. Come, come. Dine with us, and end well a day so well begun.

Ad. [*Approaching Mon.*] I know what he will say: "I must go back to town at once!" Oh, I know; he said it to me six times.

Mon. You must forgive him. Six times was a good many times for him.

Ad. Oh! I thank him for all of them, few as they were, and I love him for them, [*crosses to Oct.*] because, after all, you know he needn't have come at all. [*Takes Oct.'s hand, and kisses it.* OCT. *crosses to* R. *with Mon.*]

Mon. [*Getting Oct. towards* L. *arch.*] She is adorable. [*Aside.*] If you have another like her—bring her here, too. [*Aloud.*] Well, you will dine with us?

Oct. No, I must go back.

Mon. But why?

Oct. [*Taking his arm.*] Oh, my dear sir, I can't leave Madame Guichard for a whole day. If I can make it all right with her, perhaps I shall get back in time for dinner.

Mon. Poor prisoner! You will have a heap of gold, but you will pay a heavy price for it. Send a dispatch to Madame Guichard that you are with me. She has heard you speak of me?

Oct. Yes!—But I told her I was going down to see my uncle. [*Child follows them a step across, watching.*]

Mon. Very well! Send a dispatch to your uncle to send a dispatch to Madame Guichard. Phew! it must be very fatiguing to you to have to lie to her as a regular thing.

Oct. Oh, I'm getting used to it. [*They exit,* R. AD. *watches them out, and after looking about to see that they are alone, throws herself into the arms of Ray, who is kneeling.*]

Ad. Oh, mamma! My darling mamma!

Ray. [*Presses her hand upon Ad.'s mouth.*] Sh! [*Gently.*] Bad child, suppose they should hear you?

Ad. There's no danger. But it is so long since I saw you that I must hug you to me, I must. Oh, I love you so much, my darling mother! And now I will be able to say it to you every day and every hour. But why did you not come to me for three months?

Ray. [*Still kneeling.*] I could not, my darling, but I wrote to you many times! You got my letters?

Ad. Oh, yes! and I read and read them so many times— over and over! that was my answer. I only learned to read for your letters.

Ray. What have you done with them?

Ad. Oh, I burned them all. I learned them all by heart, and where they are written now, no one can find them. [*She places her mother's hand upon her own heart.*]

Ray. [*Embarrassed and abashed.*] Is it possible then, my child, that you understand?

Ad. I do not understand anything, mamma! I have not tried to find out anything; but I have felt—that is all—that you alone in all the world loved me, and that it is a secret. Why this is I don't know, and it does not matter, for now, my pretty mamma, [*patting her cheeks*] we can love each other all day long. I'll tell you how we'll manage it. When we are alone together, quite alone, you will be mother; when anyone else is near I will call you madame, and I shall love you all the more when I can show it the least. [*Kiss.*]

Ray. And you are certain not to betray yourself?

Ad. Oh, I'm sure. They might cut me in pieces before they could make me say what I wish to keep secret. [RAY. *kisses her.*] Nothing can separate us now, can it?

Ray. Nothing!

Ad. I shall sleep near you at night?

Ray. Yes!

Ad. [*Clapping her hands.*] In your bed-room?

Ray. In the next one to it.

Ad. With the doors open?

Ray. Yes.

Ad. [*Pleased, and joyfully.*] And the first that wakes in the morning will run in to kiss the other.

Ray. My darling! my darling!

Ad. Some one is coming! [*They listen.* RAY. *rises.*] I'll run away. [*Crosses to* R. *and comes back.*] Do you want to be ever so good to me?

Ray. What is it?

Ad. Where is your room?

Ray. There! [*Pointing* R.]

Ad. I am so tired, and I have cried and laughed so much to-day. Let me sleep in your bed. Let me roll about in your bed, won't you?

Ray. Run, then!

Ad. [*Going, returns.*] Oh!!! How I love you!

Seeing REMY, *who enters from* L.

Thanks, madame, for all your goodenss. [*Bows, then runs off,* R.]

Ray. What is it, Remy?

Remy. [L.] Why there's a lady as has come to see the lady of the house, she says, and I suppose she meant you, my lady.

Ray. [*Sits,* R.] Did she not ask for me by my name?

Rem. Well, she didn't speak the ship in the ordinary way, but she boarded right off, and backed me on to the quarter afore I could hail her.

Ray. Admit her, at all events.

Rem. Aye, aye, my lady. But I say, [*confidentially*] she carries a good many guns. [*Nods and winks.*] A regular seventy-four, full sail! all her canvas! all the flyers out! bunting at the fore, and her spanker well filled. Heavy metal, my lady—and I should judge by her figure-head—red hot shot in the furnace, and cleared for action.

Ray. Very well, my good Remy, ask her to walk in.

Rem. Aye, aye, my lady. [*Goes to door,* L., *and beckons on* Mad. G.] This way, marm!

Bows MADAME GUICHARD *in, then veers off, hitches his trousers, and goes off,* L., *shaking his head in admiration.* Mad. G. *is very richly but vulgarly dressed, and is very much excited.*

Mad. Guichard. [RAY. *rises.*] You are Captain Montaglin's wife, I believe.

Ray. Yes, madame. With whom have I the honor to speak?

Mad. G. [*Bringing chair from* L. C. *to* C.] To Madame Guichard, widow of Anatole Guichard, deceased, and the person who in three weeks will be married to M. Octave.

Ray. [*Seated at table,* R.] What can I do to serve you, madame?

Mad. G. Everything. [*Takes chair.*] First of all you can give me some information which I must have. [*Both sit.*]

Ray. Pray command me.

Mad. G. Octave came here this morning?

Ray. Yes, madame.

Mad. G. I knew it. He came here with a child about nine or ten years old.

Ray. He did.

Mad. G. I knew it. Now, where is that child?

Ray. She is asleep at present. She is very much fatigued.

Mad. G. She can't be seen, then? And her father—where is he?

Ray. Her father?

Mad. G. Yes, her father. Octave *is* her father. You know it, as well as I do.

Ray. If you will take the trouble to wait here a few minutes, madame, I will go and tell M. Octave, since it is he you have come to seek in my house.

Mad. G. Oh, yes! [*Laughs.*] I forgot I was in somebody else's house and not my own. [*Serious.*] But don't you get put out for me. My disposition is a little excitable, and to-day I have good reason for it. I havn't slept a wink all night. I've been all the morning in a cab, racing through streets, till I took the train for this place. [RAY. *half rises.*] Thanks, I don't want anything; I'm not hungry; I ate a cracker on the way. I've got nothing against you, my little lady; on the contrary, I want your help. [*Laughs, getting nearer.*] I want to know the truth about this child that Octave brought here to-day. I must know it, and I will, [*slamming upon the table*] cost what it may. [*Confidentially.*] That child has a mother. You can't make me believe she hasn't. No, no! I'm not such a fool as that. Oh, no! Now, what I want to know is: who is this mother? I want to see her, and when I do [*with a threatening, suggestive smile*]—but never mind that. It only bores you, I suppose. I'll come to the point at once. It's a short story, for when I come to the point I am a woman of very few words. [*Serious.*] It was only yesterday evening that Octave came to me, and says he in a careless sort of way: "I'm going to my uncle's at Fontainbleau to-morrow!" Well, I suspected him. I don't know why, but I did. I let him go, and I sent for Jovin.

Ray. [*Politely.*] Jovin?

Mad. G. My lawyer's clerk. Sharp as a needle. I put him on the scent, and I followed the trail myself. Two were sure to catch him. Well, my gentleman went to his house. I waited at the corner in my cab. At six o'clock this morning he came out, went to the railway station, and bought his ticket, but not for Fontainbleau. I first thought of rushing out and collaring him on the spot, and asking him if that was the way to his uncle's. But if I do, said I to myself, I will know nothing. He has deceived me, now let me find out why. Well, he went on the train: I went on the train. He got out at Rueill: I got out at Rueill. I followed him to the cottage of some poor peasants. I waited for him. I gave him ten minutes. If he hadn't come out in ten minutes I would have gone in. In eight minutes and a half he made his appearance with this child and a trunk. A little trunk. Well, I followed after my gentleman, and his little girl, and her little trunk, but I was not fast enough, and I lost the train. An hour later I was in Paris. There I met my faithful Jovin. He had taken up the chase, and tracked the man, the child, and the trunk to the Northern station. I posted him after, with orders to telegraph me every hour. Thirty minutes ago I received the message that brought me here. The rascal came to your house with the girl. Now I ask *you*, who is this child? [*Turns to face her.*]

Ray. Madame! [*Rises and crosses to* L.]

Mad. G. [R.] I understand, my dear. You think this is a matter that ought to be settled between Octave and me, and I ought not to ask you for help. I'll tell you why I do so. I've often heard him speak of you and your husband. I never thought anything of either of you till he brought this child here. Then I began to suspect, for I'm jealous. Oh, I'm frightfully jealous! [RAY. *sits,* L.] I came here to see you!! I confess it. [*Rises.*] I saw you at one of the windows before I came in. Well, I saw you were pretty, which was not very re-assuring to me. I went to the village; I talked about you. Everybody knew you, everybody praised you; I never heard such praise: you were an angel, you were a saint; you never did anything wrong, you couldn't, you wouldn't. That *was* re-assuring. Madame, I suspect no longer! I believe you to be a respectable person.

Ray. Madame!

Mad. G. [*Goes back to her seat.*] No thanks! It's your due! But to the next point. I know Octave. He's fascinating—dangerously fascinating, and I have to watch him. It's my only occupation, and I love it. It's my duty. In fact, I don't understand how anyone can love and not do it. Now, what is he here for? Why does he bring this child here? That's what I want to know. I've told you everything—tell me something! I won't let on that I heard it from you. 'Pon my word and sacred honor I won't. Tell me—do—just a little!

Ray. Madame! If I can find M. Octave—

Mad. G. Don't you know where he is? [*Rises.*] I'll soon tell you.

Ray. You have seen him?

Mad. G. Wait! [*Blows a whistle which she wears about her neck.*]

JOVIN *appears,* C.

Jovin. [*Takes off hat.*] Beg pardon—you called?
Mad. G. [*Authoritatively.*] M. Octave?

Jov. [R.] Garden yonder! Walking with the Captain!

Mad. G. [*To Ray.*] You see! [*To Jov.*] Jovin, come here.
[*He advances.*] Madame de Montaglin—M. Jovin.

Jov. [*Humbly.*] Jerome Lucien Joseph Jovin—clerk to
Jovin Brothers, Notaries.

Mad. G. [C.] If your husband ever manifests a disposition
to go and spend the day with his uncle—I recommend Jovin.

Ray. Let me go at once to M. Octave, and send him to you.
[*Crossing up to* C.]

Mad. G. See here! Don't say it's a lady who wants him.
Say a—a person. If you say a lady, he'll make up a story.

Jov. [*Aside.*] Or make over the garden wall.

Ray. I will do as you wish, madame.

Mad. G. Thank you. I'll be ever so much obliged and I'll
do as much for you any time.

Ray. Oh! [*Going.*] Let me send you some refreshments
while you are waiting. [*Exits,* R.]

Mad. G. Only a glass of beer.

Jov. [*Calling after her.*] Two glasses.

Mad. G. We have him now, Jovin!

Jov. Tricked, trapped, pinioned, hooked; in fact, caged.

MAD. G. *takes off her hat, and rolls up her lace cuffs, as* REMY
enters with tray, R.

Mad. G. Now, my fine fellow! My precious young gentleman! If you don't tell me the truth, I'm mistaken.

Remy. Please, ma'am, here's summat.

Jov. Beer! [*Smacks his lips, as he hands a glass to Mad. G.*]

Mad. G. [*Sits,* L., *and drinks it heartily, then smacks her lips.*]
Jovin, to your post.

Jov. I'm off. [*Going.*] Stop! 'Bout ship. [*To Rem., as
he is going. Takes the jug and a glass.*] Now you can go. [*Pushing him off.*] And don't listen at the keyhole.

Rem. Well, dash my binnacle! [*Exits,* R.]

Jov. Now's your chance! Don't let him up! Squeeze him!
Have it out!

Mad. G. [*Fixing herself sternly and wrathfully in chair.*] I
will—I will. [JOV. *fills a large glass and hands it to Mad. G.
Then, with an air of great satisfaction, pours out for himself; is
much disappointed in finding nothing left but froth.*]

Mad. G. [*Drinks.*] I feel better now. I'm ready for him.

Jovin. [*Looking off.*] Here he comes. I'm off. [*Exits,* C.]

QUICK CURTAIN.

ACT II.

SCENE.—*Same as last.*

MADAME GUICHARD *is discovered in the same place as at the end of Act I, finishing her glass of beer.*

MONTAGLIN *enters,* R., *first making a sign to some one, as he stands on the threshold. Then comes down to her.*

Montaglin. You wish to speak to me, madame?
Mad. Guichard. You are Captain Montaglin?
Mon. Yes, madame.
Mad. G. Your wife told you I was here?
Mon. She did.
Mad. G. I've nothing to say to you—but it's just as well, perhaps, you came. I want to see Octave.
Mon. [*Sits,* C.] Octave is gone.
Mad. G. To Paris?
Mon. To Paris.
Mad. G. Before or after Madame Montaglin told him I was here?
Mon. Before.
Mad. G. [*Rises, approaches Mon.*] Oh, Captain! You that never told a lie! How can you say that?
Mon. How do you know I never told a lie?
Mad. G. I can tell it by your face. Now own up. Octave sent you ahead to talk with me, so that he might have time to make up a story that will blind me. He has not yet left the house, but he's very near. [*Looks around.*] He's behind a door somewhere, or at a keyhole, watching me to see when it's safe to come in.

Turns, looks around, JOVIN *puts his head in,* C., *and points to* R., *nods, winks, puts his finger upon his nose, then disappears.*

He is there! [*Goes to* R.] Come out, my friend.

OCTAVE *enters,* R.

Excuse me [*to Mon.*] for treating your house like my own, but this is a very grave case. [*Stage,* L.]

Octave. [*Haughtily.*] What do you want with me, madame?

Mad. G. You are putting on your dignity because some one is present.

Mon. I think I'd better retire, madame.

Mad. G. You needn't if you don't want to, Captain. But I rather think he'd feel better if we were alone. [*Sits,* L.]

Mon. Oh, yes, it would be better. [*To Oct. in a low voice, poking him in the side, as he goes,* R.] I congratulate you. She's charming. [*Exits.*]

Oct. [R.] Now that we are alone, perhaps you'll have the goodness to tell me how you have the face to come here among people whom you never saw before, to make a scene as ridiculous as it is unpleasant. Fortunately you found the mistress of the house a lady of good breeding and good heart. Another would have had you turned out by her footmen.

Mad. G. Have you finished?

Oct. [*Sitting,* C.] What do you wish them to take you for? You forget that you are to be my wife.

Mad. G. [*Seated,* L.] What a happiness! But as we are not married yet, I shall talk to you as I please. [*Facing him.*] What girl is this?

Oct. What girl do you mean?

Mad. G. The child you brought here?

Oct. Well, it's a child.

Mad. G. Whose?

Oct. [*Sulkily.*] The daughter of a friend of mine.

Mad. G. A friend of yours. What's his name?

Oct. If he wished to be known he would have acknowledged the child.

Mad. G. Oh! And she is in your charge?

Oct. Yes. During her father's absence.

Mad. G. Why did you bring her here?

Oct. Because her father, who is also a friend of Captain Montaglin's, directed me to give her over to him.

Mad. G. Why have you never spoken to me of this child, or this friend?

Oct. Because it was a secret.

Mad. G. [*Rises and goes to him threateningly.*] You know that I don't believe a word you are saying?

Oct. [*Crossing to* L. *with careless air.*] As you please.

Mad. G. Now fooling aside. [*Speaks snappishly;* OCT. *gets further away.*] Do you hear me? Tell me the truth!

Oct. I have told it you.

Mad. G. Oh you—! [*Takes* R. H. *corner and back, assumes calmness, sits* R.] This child is yours!

Oct. [*Takes the chair,* L.] If you like it better so—so be it. She is mine.

Mad. G. Don't you dare to answer me back that way. I know it's your child. And the mother—where is she?

Oct. She is dead.

Mad. G. It's not true.

Oct. She is alive, then.

Mad. G. [*Jumps up in a rage, paces up and down.*] Oh! [*Throws herself in a chair, after taking stage, and cries with vexation.*]

Oct. [*Going to her.*] You won't believe me, so it's not my fault.

Mad. G. Why didn't you tell me you had a child? [*Weeping.*]

Oct. Because I forgot it. I cared nothing about it. [*Crosses to chair,* R.]

Mad. G. Oho, you're going to take the matter like that, are you?

Oct. I take it as I ought with a woman to whom I cannot talk as I would to any other, and who is always making her petty jealousies public—like a low-bred person.

Mad. G. [*Jumps up.*] It is true! I'm nothing! Nobody, low-bred as you say. I can hardly read and write, and I talk—the Lord knows how. That is all true. But to-day [*going to him*] I am Madame Guichard—I am a widow—I have two houses in Paris, and sixty thousand a year income! Guichard married me, he did, when I was nobody, and he never caused me a tear. [*Getting nearer to him.*] He was a true and honest man.

Oct. Well, I congratulate you on his memory.

Mad. G. [*Angrily, stage* L.] Oh you—! [*Choking, and then sarcastic.*] I suppose *she* was a woman of quality—this woman—whoever she was?

Oct. Yes.

Mad. G. Handsome?

Oct. Very.

Mad. G. [*Sighs.*] You see her sometimes? [OCT. *coolly turns his back and keeps silent—she suddenly.*] Answer me this instant, sir!

Oct. How can I see her when I tell you she is dead.

Mad. G. [*Approaching him.*] Upon your word?

Oct. Upon my word.

Mad. G. Honor?

Oct. [*Without hesitation.*] Honor!

Mad. G. [*Pleased, aside.*] I'm glad she's dead. [*Sighs; a pause.*] You loved her?

Oct. Yes. [OCT. *unobserved by her, watches her countenance to see the effect of his replies, and maliciously enjoying her distress.*]

Mad. G. [*Bitingly.*] Much?

Oct. Very much.

Mad. G. [*Almost inclined to slap him.*] How long?

Oct. Until she died.

Mad. G. [*Looking away, sympathizing, then.*] Tut! tut! and how long is it since that?

Oct. About two years.

Mad. G. [*Angry again.*] Since you knew me?

Oct. Yes.

Mad. G. Then you used to see her?

Oct. Rarely. She was sick. She wouldn't see any one, and couldn't go out.

Mad. G. And all those two years you deceived me when you told me you never loved anybody but me. [*Throws herself into chair,* C.] Oh, dear! You've been like all the rest.

Oct. Yes, unfortunately.

Mad. G. Three years you have known me, and never betrayed the secret. Ah, well! You are too much for me. I shall never have faith in you again. [*Rises.*] I who believed every word you said to me. What will become of me? [*Weeps in her hands, then takes out handkerchief and wipes her eyes, then sits unhappily, tapping her foot. Feigns hysterics, peeps out one side of handkerchief to watch the effect.* OCT. *watches her. After a pause she drops her handkerchief;* OCT. *takes his hat, and goes over to her, picks up the handkerchief, and wipes her eyes.*]

Oct. Well, good-bye! [*Assuming melancholy air.*]

Mad. G. Good-bye? [*Suddenly stops crying, and speaks in amazement.*] What do you mean?

Oct. You were right. We ought never to meet again. I leave you forever.

Mad. G. You leave me forever. And what am I to do?

Oct. I give you your liberty. May you be happy. [*Going up,* C.]

Mad. G. My liberty! What shall I do with it? [*Ill temperedly banging her elbow on table and hurting herself.*]

Oct. I don't know, but we must part.

Mad. G. We must?

Oct. [*Affecting sincerity.*] Yes, for there is too decided a difference in our circumstances for us ever to be happy together. It is not your fault. You cannot change. For a long time I wanted to tell you the whole truth about this—little affair—

Mad. G. [*Echoing and indicating by her hand a growing child.*] Little affair!—

Oct. But I was afraid you would not take kindly to the poor little one.

Mad. G. I?

Oct. You. How could I tell how far jealousy would lead you. So I thought it best to be silent. You would not under-stand. You've neither refinement nor delicacy. Ah well! We can't be happy together—let us part while we may. If we married in this humor, we should hate each other for the rest of our lives.

Mad. G. Ah, how well you know that I cannot give you up. Miserable that I am—what a slave is my heart. I am a fool, for you lead me wherever you will—and I love you—oh! I love you too much. [*Crosses* R. *Rising to the height of love and anger, she drops on his shoulder.*]

Oct. You! You don't love me at all. [*Crosses* L. MAD. G. *very angry.* OCT. *takes her seat at* L. H. *table.* MAD. G. *approaches him as she speaks.*]

Mad. G. Do not abuse your power. My friend, do not, I tell you, do not!—Because if it ever come that I can tear you from my heart and treat you like a foe, it will be a sore day for you. Pshaw! Let us finish what we were talking about. You say the mother of this child is dead. Is that true? [*Standing over him.*]

Oct. I have given you my word.

Mad. G. [*Resuming her cheerfulness.*] Well, go and get the child. Bring her to me; I will take her. She shall be mine.

Oct. [*Rises, amazed and stunned.*] You—you will take her!

Mad. G. Yes. You shall not have any cause to say I do not love you. This is what I propose—accept or not, as you please, but I give you my word: the word of a woman without refinement and delicacy:—that I will not marry you unless I can have your child in my house with me! Then if the mother lives—I shall know!! Let her come to me—I will have my answer ready.

Oct. [*Who has recovered, but is anxious.*] But why give yourself this trouble?

Mad. G. It pleases me to do it. Why do you force this trouble on strangers? It is only natural your daughter should live with us.

Oct. Certainly! But—

Mad. G. But what?

Oct. Captain Montaglin will consider all this very extra-ordinary. Besides, I think it better the child should remain here.

Mad. G. You think I would bring her up rather badly, eh?

Oct. No, I didn't say that.

3

Mad. G.   No, but you insinuated as much.

Oct.   I really did not intend.

Mad. G.   Yes, you did. [*A short quarrel, and quick exchange of words.*]

Oct.   Hold your tongue. You're always talking. I can't get in a word.

Mad. G.   Make yourself easy—if I don't understand Spanish and Italian, there are teachers who do, and she shall have the best. [*Sits* R.]

Oct.   I shall look like one who is led about as a baby at his nurse's apron. [*Approaching her.*] My dear, you must think of my feelings—my self-respect.

Mad. G.   There's no question of self-respect—it's paternal affection.

Oct.   Yes, but people don't come to friends and beg them to take charge of a child—then, two hours after, take it away again.

Mad. G.   Oh, they'll understand. Besides, they haven't had time in these two hours to become attached to her; and more than that, if they have her interest at heart they'll be delighted to hear that I intend to adopt her. It is the little one's fortune. [*Rising and looking at her watch.*] What time is it? [*Contemplatively.*] Humph! Half an hour to get to Paris. An hour to do what I wish.

Oct.   [L.] What are you going to do in Paris?

Mad. G.   It does not concern you.

Oct.   Tell me at least.

Mad. G.   No. You will find out when I get back. I will be back between three and four, with my carriage, and we will take the child with us.

Oct.   Not to-day.

Mad. G.   Why not?

Oct.   Because Montaglin leaves to-morrow, and has asked me to dinner with him to-day. I've accepted and can't refuse now.

Mad. G.   [R. H.] Of course not—we will all dine together. He'll invite me.

Oct.   I doubt it.

Mad. G.   We'll see! To-night he and I will be the best friends in the world. You stay here—tell them my resolution. When I come back I will apologize for going without taking leave of them. You see, I know what etiquette is—if I had only time to practice it. [*Goes.*] Oh! I forgot! [*Gets* L. *of Oct.,* whistles.]

Jovin *enters* c., *looks furtively at* Oct., *who looks at him surprised.*

Jovin. [R.]   You called me?

Mad. G.   Yes.   I'm going to Paris.   I won't need you any longer.   Stay.   Don't let me forget my manners.   Octave, my dear, you don't know this gentleman?

Oct. [L.]   No.   Who is he?

Mad. G.   Jovin!   Clerk to my notaries.   He knows you. Ha! ha!   He followed you all day in a cab.   [*Both laugh at Oct.*]

Oct.   What?   Then it's to this gentleman I'm indebted for the morning's surprise, is it?   You rascally—

Jov.   Look here!   Look here!   [*Gets behind Mad. G.*]   Keep him off.

Oct.   Rascal!

Mad. G.   I helpèd him.   If you forgive me, you must him. As I said before, you can return to Paris.   Will you go with me?

Jov. [L.]   Thank you; but Captain Montaglin and I have become such very good friends that I'm asked to dinner.

Mad. G.   Good!   I'll be back and make one of the party.

Jov.   I'll see you to the gate.

Mad. G.   [*Crosses to* L.]   And we can settle your bill on the way.

Jov.   Bill!   Madame, I have no bill.   What I have done was commenced as a lawyer, but is finished as a friend.   Say to me "Lucien Jerome Joseph, I thank you!" and the balance is struck.

Mad. G.   No, no, not struck, [*slapping him violently on the back*] for I shall always owe you a debt of gratitude.   Bye, bye, Octave; take care of yourself, my lad!   [*Exits;* Oct. *kissing his hand to her.*]

Jov.   [*Imitating tone.*]   Bye, bye, sir!

Oct.   What!   You—

Jov.   Oh!   [*Retreats precipitately after Mad. G.*]

Oct.   [*Alone.*]   She doubts nothing, suspects nothing more. Now to induce Raymonde to give up Adrienne.   She must, or we are both lost.

RAYMONDE *enters,* R.

Raymonde.   [*With a gasp of satisfaction.*]   I have just seen that woman leave here.   What did she come for?   What does she want?

Oct.   She wants to give me a proof of her affection—and so she has offered to adopt Adrienne.

Ray. And you refused?

Oct. I have consented, and I was about to let you know.

Ray. You wish to take Adrienne back from me?

Oct. I will bring her to you from time to time.

Ray. [*Going* L.] It is useless. Find some other means, make some other plan.

Oct. There is no other way. Think a moment, and you will see how serious your position is. Your honor is at stake, [RAY. *drops into seat,* L.] and I care for it in spite of your injustice to me. Madame Guichard is uneducated, but she lacks neither penetration nor spirit. If she were to suspect that you were the mother, her jealousy would rouse the worst of her traits. She would have but one idea: to revenge herself on me, and on you; grossly, brutally, irreparably. She would break off our marriage—of course, you don't care for that; but she would also tell your husband all that she had discovered. I would have to fight him, and he would kill me, or I would kill him. [RAY. *starts, and looks at him.*] Of course, I should do my best not to be killed. Everyone for himself.

Ray. Have you not done me injury enough in your life?

Oct. I don't do this! It is fate. Come, take my advice. [*Taking his chair towards her.*] Let us commence by gaining time. Once your husband is gone, we shall have less to fear, and can devise other means.

Ray. [*Not able to stay her tears any longer.*] You are right!

Oct. Good! [*Sits.*] Well, then listen. Madame Guichard is very changeable. She will soon become weary of the child, and some fine day will give it back to you with pleasure. I undertake on my side to do the best to bring it about.

Ray. [*Rises.*] When must I give up my child?

Oct. [*Rises.*] She will return for her at four o'clock. [*Takes his hat from* R. *table, and goes up.*]

Ray. I must prepare Adrienne for it; otherwise she will betray herself. We cannot expect, although she is your child, her father's presence of mind. If she betray herself, my husband will know all. You, that are so cool and ready, go—find Monsieur de Montaglin, and keep him away as long as you can. For while I speak to Adrienne he must not see her tears nor mine. Go, it is the last service I shall ask at your hands.

Oct. Keep cool! Keep cool, and rely on me.

Ray. I thank you. [*He exits at the back.*]

Ray. [*Alone, getting* R.] I am lost! As wife or as mother I am lost! Oh, how soon we become used to happiness. [*Sits,* R.] For mine is but two hours old, and I began to think it would last forever. Heaven meant it for my punishment. It is but just. But my child must be saved. Let me suffer, I who am guilty, but not she, that is innocent. She shall not be given to this woman, [*Rises nervously.*] who loves her not, who detests her, perhaps, and who will revenge on *her* everything *she* is made to suffer by her husband. [*Stage,* L.] What shall I do? Fly with Adrienne? [*Running* C.] And my husband, who gave me his name, and who believes in me, who relies on me for the repose of his old age; him whom I respect and love! Dishonor him! No! No! [L. *again. Sits* L. *table, overcome.*] Oh, but if I tell him all he will despise me, he will drive me from his door. Oh, Almighty Power, pity—pity—pity me! [*Sinks on floor, kneeling, burying her head in her hands. Pause; then looking up, brushing away her tears.*] I do well to talk, to weep, to tremble. [*Rising.*] Is there any power in the world that can take my child from me, while I live. What care I for myself! *She* must be saved—let what will come afterwards to me. [*Goes to door,* R.]

ADRIENNE *runs out to her.* RAY. *drops on her knees as she meets the child and folds her to her heart.*

Ray. My darling! my darling! who shall take you from me? [*Then calmer.*] Did I wake you? [*Both get* L., RAY. *sits.*]

Adrienne. No, mamma. Oh, how nicely I slept! And what nice dreams I had, all of you, dear mamma. [*Arms round Ray.'s neck.*]

Ray. Dear child! You only think of me.

Ad. Of whom should I think?

Ray. Listen to me attentively. You told me that you were brave and strong.

Ad. Yes. What must I do?

Ray. We must be separated for a little while. Try and prepare yourself for the parting.

Ad. But we will see each other again?

Ray. Yes. Very soon. I promise that.

Ad. Where must I go?

Ray. Never mind where. Now attend to me well. A lady will come here to-day; you don't know her; she is going to be the wife of Monsieur Alphonse. This lady wishes to take you away with her.

Ad. [*Becoming sad.*] But I don't want her to!

Ray. Nor I, my own darling. But to-day you must pretend to like this lady very much, and make believe you will do everything she wishes; you must even make believe that you are glad to go with her, and then she will consent that you may stay with me till to-morrow. To-morrow you will have nothing to fear from her.

Ad.   And what am I to do next?

Ray.   Next—as you are brave and wise, and as you love me—

Ad.   Oh, mamma! [*Loving her.*]

Ray.   And as nobody must know for a very long time what has become of you—as I even must seem not to know—you will leave this house all alone, when nobody sees you, and then go back to Paris, and to the house of my old nurse at Montmartre. [AD. *sinks slowly on her knees, looking up into her mother's face.*] Don't forget this; for, perhaps, I cannot talk to you alone again.

Ad.   Oh, I understand, mamma; I understand it all.

Ray.   Then you must write a letter, and leave it here, saying that you don't wish to live with me, nor with that lady. Then, as she has no right to you, she will go away, and you and I will see each other once more, never, never again to part!

Ad.   I'll remember all, dear mamma! Montmartre—at your old nurse's! I know. As for the lady, [*laughs*] she may be sure that I will adore her as much as she wants—until to-morrow. [*Kiss.*] What is the name of your old nurse, mamma?

Ray.   Mother Simon! I will give you a letter to her.

Ad.   [*Hurriedly and low.*] Monsieur is coming!

MONTAGLIN *enters from* R.

Montaglin.   [*Kindly taking the child by the hand.*] Why, Raymonde, you have been weeping.

Ray.   I? No.

Mon.   Your eyes are all red. What is the matter?

Ray.   This poor child has told me how sad and how unfortunate she has been until now.

Mon.   [*To Ad., turning the child to* R.] Stay in your room a little while, my darling. I have to speak a moment to Madame de Montaglin.

Ray.   [*Aside.*] Heaven! What is he about to say?

Ad.   Yes, sir! Good bye!

Mon.   Not good bye! Only for a little while. [AD. *exits,* R., *watching Ray.'s look.*]

Mon.   Has Octave told you that his wife consents to adopt this child? [*Sits,* C.]

Ray.   He told you, too!

Mon.   Yes.

Ray.   [*Aside, seated,* L.] Miserable!

Mon. It is the best thing that could happen for the little creature.

Ray. Do you think so? Do you believe the child can ever be happy with this father who never loved her, and this woman who never saw her? Who knows if this creature, uneducated, ignorant, violent, and jealous, does not intend to make the unhappy little one suffer a martyrdom?

Mon. Oh no! I don't think Madame Guichard has a bad heart.

Ray. The child herself trembles with fear. We were speaking of it as you came in. At my first words she burst in tears, and in terms so touching supplicated me to keep her with us.

Mon. It cannot be done. Madame Guichard has made it the express condition of her marriage. Who knows, it may be the redemption of the child. Simple and uneducated natures, like this woman's, are capable of all excesses, in goodness as well as the rest. Besides, she is rich and generous. Adrienne's future happiness is, perhaps, secure with her. [*Rises.*] At all events, we cannot oppose the will of her father. He gave her to us this morning, he takes her away this evening. It is his right, and his duty as well. As it is the only time he has ever done that duty—perhaps, we ought not to reproach him.

Ray. But, if the child does not wish to go with this woman?

Mon. She will have to obey.

Ray. [*Rises.*] What right has this man?

Mon. We only know what he tells us about that. And no matter how little right he has—he has more than we.

Ray. I fear him! I feel that he will cause her some great misfortune. [*Crosses to* R.]

Mon. How? Why?

Ray. [R., *with warmth and growing feeling.*] Because the child told me but now, here, that she would rather beg her bread, that she would rather die of frost and hunger, than live with Monsieur Alphonse, as she calls him, and with this stranger! Poor little outcast, her infancy has been so sad, so lonely: a violent grief now would kill her. See how pale she is, how delicate! Think what it is to have no father, no mother! to live one's childhood with ignorant and brutal peasants, who keep her only for the money she brings them; who would have sold her to this woman that dogged the steps of her future husband, if he had not thought of bringing her here. And he! Miserable being! More selfish than they, he sells her to the creature at her own price. And you—you! the best of men, you think it right! and you will not defend this little struggling creature against him, at the very moment that she commences to live, to breathe, when her pent-up heart commences to grow and to rejoice! Oh, there is, there must be some justice against such infamy as this!! [*Crosses to* L.]

Mon. [*Watches her attentively to the end, and then as she ceases to speak and crosses from him, he seizes her arm.*] Raymonde! [*She looks at him, and then in affright she starts back.*] I begin to understand!!

Ray. [L., *still frightened and slowly.*] To understand!! What?

Mon. The truth!! [*Looks fiercely at her; she stands appalled.*]

Ray. The truth?

Mon. Yes. Your tears, your passion, your words wrung by despair from a heart overflowing with terror and with love, reveal all to me.

Ray. [*Throwing herself at his feet, and clasping his hand.*] Oh, forgive me! forgive me!

Mon. [*Looks around.*] Hush! ·

Ray. I await my sentence from your lips, after I have told you all.

Mon. [*Impressive whisper.*] No. No. Say nothing.

Ray. I understand—you despise me.

Mon. No. I pity you.

Ray. But there is one thing you must hear—I did not bring Adrienne to this house. That deception was not my work. I would have suffered in secret all my life—visited my child by stealth—left her to strangers—lost her by disease and death for want of a mother's care—rather than betray your unsuspecting heart. Oh, sir! wretched as I am, I would have tried to do my duty to you! [*Sobbing and broken down, she sinks on her knees, hiding her face with her hands.*]

Mon. I believe you! [MON. *sinks into chair,* C.]

Ray. Oh then, [*rises*] listen to me, so that you may not utterly despise me. Years ago, when I was a child almost, when I had not father, nor mother, nor friend, when, like every girl, my heart longed for companionship and love—I saw one who offered me marriage!

Mon. Marriage? [*Turning his face half towards her.*]

Ray. I accepted him. By the ceremony that took place, I believed we were man and wife. For a few short years in our obscure but happy home I bore his name. Then this dream of childhood was dispelled. I woke to find that neither law nor public justice recognized my right. I was deserted—I and my child. I hid away my grief and my shame—for guiltless as I was, I was ashamed. I asked those I knew, and they told me

that a marriage void in law was no marriage, blessed though it
might be by religion, that he was not bound, that I was not
bound—that I was free—free with my little child!! [*Tones of
painful sarcasm.*]

Mon. And he?

Ray. I besought him then to make good the evil he had
done, to keep his word. He refused. He told me his family
would not consent, that he was under age. He gave every reason but the truth—that he was weary of me, and would not.
Then my misery began. My child had to be sent from me, for
I dared not tell the truth to the old relative with whom I had
sought a home. I had to labor, not for my own support, but Adrienne's. Often I have shivered in the winter months to keep her
warm, and after all the rest slept, I have stolen from my bed and
sewed till daylight, to send money for her nourishment.

Mon Poor mother!

Ray. One by one my hopes fell away, and nothwithstand-
ing all my struggles, I saw the hand of misery come nearer to
mine. Then—you came. And for the first time I committed
a crime—the crime of betraying your confidence. I should have
refused your hand, or I should have told you all and trusted to
your honor and your love. Oh, I knew my duty well! But
my child's little fingers were pressed upon my lips, and I could
not speak. So my punishment came! These six years of terror,
of guilty secrecy! This moment, when instead of flying to your
bosom for protection, I must kneel at your feet for judgment.
[*Kneels.*]

Mon. Judgment on thee, who hast suffered so much! and
repented so deeply! Whence have I the right to judge! No, I
have but my duty to do! [*Solemnly and sternly, looking at her.*]

Ray. Yes! I await your justice.

Mon. [*Rises.*] For six years you have been a good and
faithful wife to me. [*She clutches his hand and kisses it pro-
foundly.*] Loving, obedient, kind, and gentle. You have given
me home and happiness, made my days so full of joy that every
respiration of my being has been a thanksgiving to the author
of all happiness!!

Ray. Oh that I could yield up my life in return for these
words!

Mon. In the eyes of the world you are guilty. [RAY. *sinks
again.*] Heaven help the weak!—guilty of not protecting yourself against the wicked and the strong. What does the world
say is my duty?—To vindicate this wrong to social laws, and bid
you kindly but firmly—Farewell! To count into your hands a
generous sum as payment for these six years of gentle service
and devotion, and as provision for your future.

Ray. It is just! It is just!

Mon. And what says my conscience, on which rests the oath I took before Heaven to love, protect, and cherish you for good, for evil, come what may? What says my heart, on which rests the debt of all these years of duty, love, and honor? They tell me I cannot break that oath when the time has come to test it! I cannot pay that debt but by years to come of love and care! Raymonde! My wife!! Here, in this home which you have made, shall you stay! Here, in this heart which you have blessed, shall you dwell! Come! To my arms!!

Ray. Oh, my husband!—my savior!

Mon. My wife!

ADRIENNE *runs in, and he clasps her to his breast.*

You and your child! She shall be mine, as you are mine! Thus do I keep the solemn promise which makes men and women one! Come good, come ill! Come what may! Thou art mine, to death and beyond! Mine! My wife!! [RAY. *throws herself into his arms with a scream of joy.*]

CURTAIN.

ACT III.

SCENE—*Same as the last.—Towards Evening.*

REMY *enters at the rise of the curtain, followed by* JOVIN, *from the garden.*

Remy. [L.] The Captain's orders was to fetch you here, so you'd better drop anchor, and wait till he puts off from shore to you.

Jovin. [R.] The Captain wants me? I say, it isn't dinner, is it? Because I never heard the bell.

Rem. Dinner! Lord love you, no. We don't have dinner yet, not till eight bells.

Jov. What is it then? What does he want me for? The lady hasn't got back yet, has she?

Rem. I don't know what the orders to the fleet is, I only knows I was sent to hail you. When I left the Captain, he was overhauling his log at the table there; but he's weighed anchor now, I see, and run into some cove hard by. [*Crosses to* R.]

Jov. Look here, my marine friend, can't you put your ideas into ordinary language that a man can understand?

Rem. Why so I do, don't I? I puts 'em into the natural lingo that all the world speaks, except the few lubbers what lives ashore, and ain't eddicated up to the commonest conversation.

Jov. What a self-satisfied old barnacle he is. Well, I suppose I'm to wait here till the Captain comes.

Rem. Aye, aye! that you are, and here he is.

MONTAGLIN *enters from* R.

Montaglin. Ah, Monsieur Jovin. [*Shakes hands, and comes down* C. *with him.*] Don't go, Remy. [*To* Rem., *who was about to exit.*] I shall want you, perhaps.

Rem. [R.] All right, Captain.

Mon. [*To* Rem.] If that lady who was here a short time ago returns, as she will shortly—you know her?

Rem. I'd pick her out of a whole fleet, if she was new rigged and painted; there's no mistaking her build, Captain.

Mon. Well, when she comes bring her to me; not to my wife, mind, but to me.

Rem. Aye, aye, Captain.

Mon. And, by the way, go outside, in the garden, and see if you can find [*with an effort*] Monsieur Octave. Ask him to step this way.

Rem. I seed him just before I towed the other gentleman in. I'll bear down on him. [*Exits, down* c.]

Mon. [*To Jov.*] I think you told me this morning, Monsieur Jovin, that you were the chief clerk of a notary, your uncle.

Jov. Yes, sir. Two of 'em, both uncles. Jovin Brothers.

Mon. I wish your assistance in a little matter involving some legal forms.

Jov. Certainly, sir, certainly. It's in my way.

Mon. I wish you to draw up the necessary documents by which a parent recognizes at law a child that—hem—you understand?

Jov. I think I do. A child that—ahem—otherwise would not be recognizable as anybody's in particular.

Mon. Yes.

Jov. Nothing easier. All in my line, exactly. I do it every day.

Mon. Ahem!

Jov. I mean drawing the papers.

Mon. What is to be done first?

Jov. Is it to be the father or the mother who recognizes the child?

Mon. The father.

Jov. Well, if the father is unmarried, and of full age, all he has to do is to sign a declaration. If he be married, he must get the consent of his wife to the act.

Mon. Good.

Jov. The child was registered at birth, I suppose, in the proper office?

Mon. Yes.

Jov. In the usual form—father and mother unknown.

Mon. Exactly.

Jov. We don't allude to the mother in the document, I suppose? Only the father?

Mon. Only the father.

Jov. You know, however, that if the mother turns up afterwards, she can attack the document as not being made by the real father.

Mon. She won't attack this one.

Jov. So far so good. Where is the registry of the child?

Mon. Here it is. [*Produces paper.*]

Jov. [*Reads.*] Sex—feminine. Registered under the name of Adrienne Marie Pauline. Father and mother unknown. August, 1864." Everything in order, sir. When shall I draw the paper? [*Getting to table,* L.]

Mon. Now.

Jov. What is the father's name?

Mon. Leave that blank for the present.

Jov. Is he married or single?

Mon. [*Rises, puts chair near back of table.*] Leave that blank, also.

Jov. All right. [*Goes to table.*]

Mon. You have the stamped paper?

Jov. Never travel without it. [*Takes out an enormous pocket-book.*] Ha! ha! the boys in the office say I carry my desk about with me. They will have their joke, sir.

Mon. Evidently. Will you go to work at once?

Jov. Yes. But to make it regular, there should be another notary with me. [*Sits.*]

Mon. Can't you dispense with that?

Jov. Yes, if you will get two witnesses.

Mon. I'll find the witnesses. As many as you want.

Jov. Two will do. [OCTAVE *coming up steps,* C.]

Mon. Leave that to me. You go to work and prepare the document while I speak with this gentleman.

Jov. [*Steps* C.] I'm at it!

As OCTAVE *enters,* JOV. *moves to the farthest end of the table, back to audience, and gets to work.* OCT. *enters* C., *glares at Jov. and comes down, puts hat on* L. *table.*

Octave. [*Looking anxiously and nervously at Mon.*] You sent for me, Captain?

Mon. [R. *After a silence, wherein is seen how great is his effort to be calm in Oct.'s presence.*] Yes, I wished to speak with you.

Oct. [*Re-assured by his tone.*] I'm at your service.

Mon. I've spoken to my wife about giving up the child to Mad. Guichard.

Oct. Ah! And she sees, I hope, the wisdom of it.

Mon. No, she does not.

Oct. How is that? You agreed with me when I spoke of it.

Mon. Yes, but women have their own ideas. Raymonde has become greatly attached to the child.

Oct. What, already?

Mon.   Already.

Oct.   In two hours?

Mon.   Good hearts are prompt to feel.

Oct.   Hem! [*Getting anxious.*] Then, I suppose that Madame de Montaglin—

Mon.   Refuses absolutely to give up Adrienne.

Oct.   But her reasons? She must have some reason.

Mon.   Don't worry about that. She has reasons, and they are not bad ones. In the first place she declares you do not love this child.

Oct.   [c.] How does she know?

Mon.   Your child does not know you even by your own name. She calls you Monsieur Alphonse. Your falsehoods began with her, at her cradle. You have been to see her but five or six times in her life; you brought her here to get rid of her, and you now demand her back, only because Madame Guichard makes it a *sine qua non* of her marriage! At this moment the child represents 50,000 a year to you; and that's the reason you want her. But if to-morrow, your wife, who seems to be as capricious as she is violent and peremptory, should take an aversion to the child, and order you to turn her out of your house, you would turn her out as coolly as you've done everything else that concerns her. Madame de Montaglin, therefore, has reason to believe that the child will be happier with her than with anybody else, and is resolved to keep her.

Oct.   [*Crosses to* R.] These are reasons! But I have my rights.

Mon.   What rights?

Oct.   I am her father.

Mon.   How will you prove it?

Oct.   I declare it now.

Mon.   That is no proof. The child has been registered: father and mother unknown. She is no more yours than anybody's.

Oct.   [*Angrily.*] Then you will become the accomplice in this act of—

Mon.   Eh?

Oct.   [*Subsiding, getting to table,* R.] I mean—you approve your wife's conduct, and encourage her in keeping Adrienne from me?

Mon.   I merely do my duty. The circumstances being as I have stated, I only have to enquire, what is my duty? Is it to protect a child that has no family, or to give her back to a stranger, who, having at first treated her as a mere clog, now wishes to use her as a speculation. I shall protect this orphan!

My conscience will be satisfied, and her future assured. But, since you affirm that you are the father of this orphan, prove it! Recognize her legally.

Jov. [*Rises, forward.*] There you are, sir. Done!

Mon. All right, my dear M. Jovin, we shall be ready for you in a moment.

Jov. Very good, sir! [*Bends over the table, correcting the document.*]

Oct. Recognize her legally! It is a very serious matter. What will my wife say to it?

Mon. That is your concern.

Oct. Let us wait till she comes, and I'll ask her.

Mon. No. Give me your answer now. Here is the notary. [*Oct. glares at Jov., who advances with the paper.*] Remy and I will be witnesses. It is a matter of five minutes. If your wife consents to take the girl, she will consent to let her bear your name.

Oct. I'm not so sure of that. Let us wait till she comes.

Mon. You refuse?

Oct. Now—yes.

Mon. Enough! [*To Jov.*] I am ready for you.

Jov. The paper is here. [*Goes to table,* L.]

Mon. [*Calling at* C. *steps.*] Remy!

REMY *enters.*

Remy. [*Loudly, as he comes up.*] Aye, aye, Captain.

Mon. Call Madame.

REMY *goes to door,* R. RAYMONDE *enters,* R.

Rem. Is that all, Captain?

Mon. No, stay here. Listen to what transpires, so that you may understand.

Rem. Is it a yarn, Captain? I see the lawyer there unreeling. [*Gets* L.]

Mon. Sh! [*To Jov.*] My dear M. Jovin, will you be good enough to read the instrument you have just drawn up.

JOV. *takes the* C. *with important air;* REM., *at* C. R., *after taking a fresh quid, puts his hand to his ear, very intent.* OCT. R. C., *and* MON. *and* RAY. L.

Jov. [*Reading.*] Before Jovin, notary, appeared Monsieur —[*stops, to Mon.*] I left the name in blank, as you desired.

Mon.   Put in mine.

Jov.   [*Goes to table.*]   Give it to me in full.

Mon.   John Mark de Montaglin.

Jov.   There! [*Reads.*]   Appeared John Mark de Montaglin, who by these presents does voluntarily and freely acknowledge for his own daughter Adrienne Marie Pauline—

Oct.   [*Surprise, steps forward.*]   You! [*To Mon.*]

Mon.   Wait a little.

Jov.   Adrienne Marie Pauline, born at Paris, August 11th, 1864, and registered in the books of records of the 8th Arondissement as born of a father and mother unknown.   And therefore the said John Mark de Montaglin does hereby consent that the said Adrienne Marie Pauline shall for the future bear the name of Montaglin; that a minute of this act shall be recorded in all places where it shall be necessary, and shall be noted on the margin of the registry of her birth.   Madame de Montaglin, wife of the said John Mark de Montaglin, hereby consents to the foregoing, and in testimony thereof has signed these presents. [*Looks at Ray.*]   That is the usual form—Do you consent? [*Bows to Ray.*]

Raymonde.   Yes.

Jov.   Done and executed in the presence of— What are the names of the witnesses? [*Looks at Rem., presenting pen, who sheers off suspiciously. MON. signs, then RAY.*]

Mon.   [R. C.]   Your name, Remy.

Rem.   [L. C.]   What does he want it for?

Mon.   It's quite right.

Rem.   There was a mate of mine once, as give his name to a lawyer arter a little bit of a frolic, and he went to jail soon arter for six months.

Jov.   I assure you, my friend, there is no danger here.   This is what we call a civil proceeding.

Rem.   Oh! Well, why didn't you say so! I'll meet any civil man half way.   Put me down Remy Benedict Deschamps, Junior.   Be particular, young man, about the spelling.

Jov.   Trust to me.

Rem.   Put me a big letter there.

Jov.   Why that's the end of the word.

Rem.   Ah! I got it upside down, didn't I?   [REM. *looks over him, and then signs an X.*]

Jov.   And the second witness?

Mon.   Monsieur Octave!

Oct.   [*Starts.*]   I? [*Down R., to Mon.*]   Why do you wish this?

Mon.   [*Gazing him steadily in the eye, then low to him.*]   Because, as Adrienne is the daughter of my wife, [Oct. *starts.*] she ought to have no father but me. [*Picks up the pen, and gives it to him.*] Sign !! [Oct. *slowly signs.*]

Ray. [*Aside,* R.] What will come of this?

Jov. All is done! Complete and exact! [*Folds up the paper.*]

Mon. [*To Ray., crosses to her.*] My dear wife, I thank you before all here for having consented to my doing this act of justice to my child. [*Kisses her forehead.*] And for having consented to accept her in your house as your own as well as mine. [*To Jov., who gives him the paper.*] Thanks, my dear sir !

Jov. That is all for the present ?

Mon. All! You stop and dine with us, of course.

Jov. Certainly! I shall have the honor and the pleasure. [*Aside.*] There is evidently a little family talk to be talked over here, and I had better go back to the goeseberries.

Rem. [C., *up a little.*] Shall I tow your honor to a new part of the garden?

Jov. My marine friend, steam ahead, I'll follow in your wake.

Rem. Now you talks! [*Exit,* C.]

Jov. [*Aside.*] Who'd suspect that fine looking old boy of having such a secret. Adrienne Marie Pauline! Well, well, there's no trusting to appearances after that. [*Exits,* C.]

Mon. [*To Ray.*] My darling, may I ask you to look to our daughter?

Ray. [*Aside to him.*] You are about to speak to that man. Oh, for the sake of Heaven, do not quarrel ! Let me suffer, not you !

Mon. Fear nothing. [*He conducts her to door,* R.*; she exits.* Mon. *then stands at the door, looking at Oct.*]

Oct. [*Gloomily.*] I am at your orders, sir.

Mon. What do you wish me to understand by that?

Oct. That I am ready to give you satisfaction.

Mon. I suppose you mean in the usual way ?

Oct. As you please.

Mon. [R.] That would not mend the affair! Your death or mine in a duel would compromise a woman who must not be involved in a single suspicion. It would moreover tell to the curious and the malignant what should be forever a secret among us three alone. As for me, I have already forgotten. As for you, you do not exist on the earth, as far as I am concerned. We shall never meet again. If by chance I shall ever see you, I shall not recognize you. When Madame Guichard returns, I

4

will receive her; and as she, above all, should not know the truth,
I will explain everything to her in such way as to appear under
obligations to you. You told me that you began with her by
saying that this child belonged to a friend of yours. I am that
friend. To save the honor of the lady you have wronged, and I
have married, I will assist in this falsehood. As for the chastise-
ment you deserve—Heaven will take care of it. I am quite
satisfied on that point. ·

Oct. Let me say that I understand nothing of all you have
done, why—

Mon. I am not surprised. You do not and never will understand the course of an honest man! You and I do not speak the
same tongue. We are not of the same species.

JOVIN *enters hastily, steps* C.

Jovin. Madame Guichard is coming! I saw her enter the
gate. Her carriage has just drawn up outside. I thought you'd
like to know.

Mon. Thank you.

Jov. [C.] You see, I thought that—

Mon. [*Impatiently.*] Exactly.

Jov. [*Running to Oct.*] Anyhow I knew you'd want to be
prepared for—

Oct. [*Angrily.*] Silence!

Jov. Oh! [*Goes up.*]

Mon. [*To Oct.*] Go into the conservatory. Let me speak
with her. After that, give her your arm, and conduct her back
to Paris. When she leaves this house, remember, the door is
forever closed upon you.

Oct. We shall see! [*Pushes Jov. aside, as he exits up stairs
into conservatory.*]

Jov. Perhaps I had better go.

Mon. [*Getting* R.] Perhaps you'd better remain.

Jov. [*Aside.*] I'm glad of that. It begins to be interesting.
And I wish to see that no one gets the advantage of my rattle-
brained client. Poor woman!

MADAME GUICHARD *enters,* L., *boisterously, as if in her own
house; throws her hat on table.*

Madame Guichard. Ah, Captain! Hello, Jovin! Where is
Octave?

Mon. Not very far.

Mad. G. I must see him at once.

Mon. What is the matter?

Mad. G. I have come for him and Adrienne, as we arranged.

Jov. Now for it.

Mon. I am sorry, madame, that you have taken so much trouble. We intend to keep Adrienne with us.

Mad. G. And I am sorry, Captain, that you have come to . that conclusion, [*sits,* L.] because when I take a thing into my head, I never give it up. I went to Paris resolved to adopt the child, as much for her sake as my own. When I got to Paris, I found out that Octave had practiced still another deception on me, and I thereupon put in execution immediately an intention I would otherwise not have carried out for some time yet.

Mon. [R.] What new deception did you discover?

Mad. G. He told me that the mother of this girl was dead.

Mon. Well?

Mad. G. Well, she is not dead.

Mon. How—how do you know that?

Mad. G. Simplest thing in the world. I sent a man to the cottage of the peasants where Adrienne was brought up.

Mon. Well, what did you do then?

Mad. G. [*Triumphantly.*] What did I do? I said to myself, she shall never see her child again. If she wishes to get her, let her come to me, [*rises*] for I am the mother now.

Mon. You the mother now? I don't understand.

Mad. G. It's simple. The law is a very good thing sometimes. To be sure, it allows people who have children to disown them, but it also allows people who have no children to adopt other people's. I have taken a bold step. I went to my notaries—

Jov. My uncles—

Mad. G. Exactly. [*Crosses to* C.] And I executed an instrument, acknowledging Adrienne Marie Pauline, father and mother unknown, born August 11th, 1864, to be my child. Here is the document. [*Flourishes it in triumph.*]

Jov. [*Crosses to* C.] Let me see it. [*Runs it over.*] Done! and no mistake.

Mad. G. [*To Mon.*] How's that?

Mon. [*After a pause.*] Well, it amounts to nothing.

Mad. G. You heard Jovin say it was all right.

Mon. Oh yes, but it can be disputed.

Mad. G. [*Serious.*] By whom?

Mon. The father.

Mad. G. Oh, he'll be glad enough of this.

Mon. Don't be too sure.

Mad. G. [*Seated,* L.] I know Octave. He'll be delighted.

Mon.   Octave is not the father of Adrienne.

Mad. G.   Octave not the father? Why he confessed it.

Mon.   But you must remember, he told you first she was the daughter of one of his friends.

Mad. G.   Yes, but that was false.

Mon.   No. You wouldn't believe it, that's all. So he determined to punish your jealousy, and so he made up a story of which not a word was true. In short, Octave has merely rendered a service to his friend, that is all.

Mad. G.   [*Pause, thinking.*]   Who is this friend?

Mon.   It is I?

Mad. G.   [*Rises.*]   You!! Captain!! But the proof?

Mon.   The proof? Why I have acknowledged the girl as my child.

Mad. G.   You have acknowledged her?

Mon.   Not half an hour since. Here is my document. [MAD. G. *grasps it, devours it; turns to* JOV., *who pretends to devour it with his eyes, then hands it back.*]

Jov.   [*Gravely.*]   Evidently regular. Done and no mistake! [*Goes up.* MAD. G. *holds the two papers in blank astonishment.*]

Mon.   You will perceive that one of the witnesses is Octave himself.

Mad. G.   [*Bursts into the heartiest laughter, as the full force of the situation breaks upon her.*]   Oh! What an idea! Why you are!—But I say, Captain, I'm compromised on all the public records. I wanted to have it known all over that the child was mine, because I thought it was Octave's! But now it turns out that you are the father. And I've acknowledged that I am the mother. [*Goes, R., scratching her head.*]

Mon.   [*Quizzically.*]   Never mind. I won't say anything about the matter.

Jov.   Neither will I.

Mad. G.   [*Crosses to Jov.*]   Hush! [*Turns to Mon.*]   Except to your wife. She must understand that I am innocent. Be sure you'll tell her. As for Octave, he'll keep his mouth shut for his own sake. Well, well! How things do happen. [*Sits.*] If anybody had told me this morning that I would be on the public records as the mother of your child! Well, well, one cannot be too careful. But Octave might have prevented it all. He ought to have told me the truth.

Mon.   It was not his secret, and besides, I swore him to silence.

Mad. G.   [*Seriously.*]   But tell me one thing. Why did he bring this girl here, in your house, if you wanted to hide her existence from your wife?

Mon. [R.] Because he hit on an excellent plan by which I could always have Adrienne near me. He brought her here as his own, and begged us, as we had no children, to take her and bring her up.

Mad. G. It was very ingenious.

Jov. [*Seated* L. *of table.*] Very ingenious. Just like one of his lies, in fact.

Mad. G. Silence, Jovin! [*Laughing, sits.*] Oh, I see it all. Very good, indeed.

Mon. Yes, he helped me to practice the deception very skill- fully.

Mad. G. [*Looking at her own document.*] Yes, a little too well. But, after all, it was to render you a service. He kept your secret, and he kept his word. I'm glad of that. I'm proud of him. He can be a man, and I forgive him everything for that. [*Rises, approaches Mon.*]

Mon. [*Gravely, and looks at her interestedly.*] You love him then, very much ?

Mad. G. It sounds ridiculous for a woman of the world, like me, doesn't it ? But his love was the first I ever had in my heart. I've had a hard life of it. I was a drudge all my years till now! I needed something to love. Don't laugh at me. I'm very wicked, you think. No:—at heart I'm all right. There is only one thing disgusts me—a lie ! When I learned that the mother was alive, after he told me she was dead, I had but one thought—revenge! But when I went to the office, and saw the registry of this poor child's birth : no father, no mother—dry and cold, like the words on a gravestone!—I thought of my own childhood, it was something like that; and I felt my heart go out to this little one whom I had never seen, and whom two hours before I hated. I made a solemn vow to be good to her. Odd, wasn't it ? But that's the sort of woman I am. Then I rushed off, and bought laces, and dresses, and presents for the little creature. They are all out there in my carriage! Let her come to me, won't you, so that I can give them to her, to my daughter, [*smiles, and archly*] to our daughter ! [*With a comic sigh.*] And then I'll leave you, and go away, like a stranger who has been found out trying to poke her nose into other people's business, and you won't be bothered with me any more. Won't you let her come to me ?

Mon. [*Grasping her hand.*] Madame Guichard, you are a good and noble woman !

Mad. G. Too quick tempered, perhaps. But if I'd had a little education, and a little money at the beginning, I might have been made something of. But I thank you, Captain; what

you have said makes me feel very good.   Ah! if one in twenty
men were like you, the world might pull through yet!!

Mon. [*Laughing.*]   Strange woman!

Mad G. Will you stand up with Octave when we are
married?

Mon. [*Startled.*]   I?   Impossible!   I—I set sail to-morrow.

Mad. G.   That's true.   Well, I may come here while you are
away, to see my daughter now and then?

Mon.   Madame de Montaglin and Adrienne go with me.
[MAD. G. *looks incredulously at him.*]   I shall be absent a year
or two, and I can't bear to leave them so long.

Mad. G.   Well, no matter.   I'd like though to see Madame
de Montaglin before I go, and ask her pardon for the way I've
acted in her house.   You'll explain [*light tone*] to her [*shows
paper*] our little mistake?

Mon.   Yes.   I'll send my wife and Adrienne to you.   I—
[*Hesitates, as if about to say something more.*]   Madame Guichard,
I hope and trust that you will be happy.   You deserve to be,
and I wish it from my heart.

Mad. G.   Is there anything else you'd like to tell me?

Mon.   No:—nothing!   [*Exits,* R.]

Mad. G.   There was something else.   He seemed agitated
and embarrassed.   Why does he take his wife away with him?
No doubt, for fear the other woman should drop in to see her
child.

Jov.   [*Who has been visibly agitated during preceding, steal-
ing from one chair to another till he gets near her, now advances,
sighing heavily, hand on heart.*] `Madame!

Mad. G.   Oh!   I forgot you were there.

Jov.   Madame Guichard!   Let me take your hand.   I ad-
mire you, madame, from the bottom of my heart.

Mad. G.   There's my hand!   [*He shakes it.*]   Why, what's
the matter?

Jov.   [*His kerchief to his eyes.*]   Excuse my emotion!

Mad. G.   My poor little friend, have I hurt your feelings in
any way?

Jov.   No, madame.   No!   The softness of my heart got the
better of my head for an emotional moment, and I oozed!   But
it is over now.

Mad. G.   I'm glad you feel better.   [*Going up, turning back.*]
Will you not be Octave's best man when we are married?

Jov.   I?   Madame, pardon me if I say to you: it can never
be!   Monsieur Octave hates me, and if he did not—

Mad. G. [R.]   He shall not!

Jov.   Then for the further reason that I hate him!   I would stand up with Monsieur Octave if he were about to go to some convenient barn, and hang himself—with pleasure! I would stand up with him in mortal combat, and be shot, or shoot him—with pleasure! But when the moment comes for him to lead you to the altar, I shall be engaged in composing an epitaph for my own early, too early tomb. Farewell, madame! [*Turning his face away.*]

Mad. G. [*Catching his arm.*] Jovin! Let me look at you! You are in love!

Jov. No!

Mad. G. Yes!

Jov. No! Nothing shall wring such a confession from me. I will hide it till its proportions become too great for the narrow limits of my suffering frame: then, should an explosion take place, search among the fragments for a faithful heart—

OCTAVE *runs in gaily from conservatory,* C.

and on it you will find inscribed in ineffacable characters these words—[*Buries his face in his* L. *hand, his* R. *extended towards Mad. G.;* OCT. *comes down between them, and takes it.* JOV., *thinking he has Mad. G.'s hand, is about to kiss it, when he discovers his mistake.*]

Octave. Ah, my dear!

Jov. Beast! [*Exits hurriedly,* L.]

Mad. G. [*Aside.*] Poor little fellow! Well?

Oct. [L.] I ran here to say—

Mad. G. I know everything. I've just seen Captain Montaglin. I know his secret. But you ought to have had confidence enough in me to tell me the truth. That would have prevented what I've just gone and done.

Oct. You?

Mad. G. Yes. I've acknowledged Adrienne as my daughter at Paris, while the Captain acknowledged her here as his.

Oct. [L.] What in the world did you do that for?

Mad. G. [R.] To prove my love for you.

Oct. Goosey! What did the Captain say?

Mad. G. [*Laughs.*] Well, he seemed rather more serious about it than I thought he ought to. But tell me, do you know the mother?

Oct. What mother?

Mad. G. Adrienne's mother.

Oct. No.

Mad. G. Don't you know her name, even?

Oct. No.

Mad. G. Truly?

Oct. I know she's some woman of rank; that's all.

Mad. G. [*Getting suspicious.*] You never met her?

Oct. Where could I meet her?

Mad. G. At the cottage where the child was.

Oct. Never! Did she ever go there?

Mad. G. Yes.

Oct. How do you know that?

Mad. G. I sent a person to find out. I wanted to know all.

Oct. [*His alarm shaken off.*] I'm glad of that. Then you found that I only went there five or six times, when the Captain sent for me to go.

Mad. G. They called you Monsieur Alphonse at the cottage. Why was that?

Oct. Because I didn't wish to give my real name and address. They would have suspected—

Mad. G. [*Forcing him to look at her.*] Look at me.

Oct. Well?

Mad. G. You swear to all this?

Oct. What in the world is the matter now?

Mad. G. Will you swear to all this?

Oct. What interest would the Captain have in acknowledging a child that was not his?

Mad. G. *I* acknowledged her, and *I* never saw her! [*Crosses to* L.]

Oct. Oh you! You're a fool!

Mad. G. Perhaps I am.

Oct. Come, we must be going.

Mad. G. What's your hurry?

Oct. We can't stay here forever.

Mad. G. I thought you were invited to dinner?

Oct. Yes, but—

Mad. G. But what?

Oct. You hadn't done what you have done.

Mad. G. I have done what he ought to be eternally grateful for, and you have rendered him the greatest service in your power for all these years. Why then should we run from the house like thieves, when one of us has been asked to dinner—[*laughs*] and the other wants to be? [OCT. *goes up impatiently.* MAD. G. *aside, serious.*] What is the meaning of his impatience? There is something behind it all. Something I don't know. They have deceived me! There's another lie! [*Snuffs.*] I smell it. It's in the air. [*Stage,* L.]

RAYMONDE *enters with* ADRIENNE, R.

Raymonde. My husband, madame, has informed me of the good intentions you had with regard to this dear child, whom I shall teach to be as grateful to you, as if she were really what the law makes her. We all understand how much we owe you; and your goodness will give you much happiness hereafter.

Mad. G. You won't mind shaking hands with me, will you? [*Crosses to her.*]

Ray. With all my heart.

Mad. G. [*Aside, as she holds the hand.*] Her hand trembles.

Ray. [*With an effort.*] It only remains for me to thank this gentleman who has been so kind to the little girl, and who for her sake has been forced to tell the falsehoods which you have forgiven, I suppose, as well as I. [*Aside.*] The words choke me! [*Aloud.*] Adrienne, go and thank the gentleman, who owes you nothing, but to whom you owe everything, since this morning. [*Crosses to* L. C.]

Adrienne. [*Offering her hand to Oct.*] I thank you, Monsieur Alphonse.

Mad. G. Kiss the little girl, Octave! since you were the father up to to-day.

Observes MONTAGLIN, *who enters*, R.

Montaglin. Madame is right. Do as she says. [OCT. *kisses the child.* RAY. *turns her face away in repulsion.* AD. *returns to Ray. Mon., aside to Ray.*] Courage for a little while longer.

Ray. [*To Ad.*] And now go and kiss madame.

Ad. That I will! [*Goes to Mad. G., affecting pleasure.* MAD. G. *kneels, puts arm around the child's waist.* AD., *once in her arms, looks around wistfully to Ray.* MAD. G. *observes the action.*]

Mad. G. The child is troubled. What is the matter with her? [*Aloud.*] Did you know, my darling, that I came here to take you away?

Ad. [*Simply.*] Where to?

Mad. G. [*Gravely.*] To my house.

Ad. For how long?

Mad. G. For good and all.

Ad. Must I go with you to-day?

Mad. G. As soon as you wish.

Ad. To-morrow, then. To-day you can stay with us.

Mad. G. Are you not sorry to leave this place?

Ad. [*Pointing to Ray.*] This lady has been good to me since I came here, but since you wish to take me, and I have no father nor mother, I will go with you gladly. But you will bring me back sometimes?

Mad. G. You love me a little?

Ad. I love you already. [*Kisses her.*]

Mad. G. Don't say that, because I shall regret you too much; for I'm going to tell you the truth now. You shall always stay here with this lady and gentleman. [*Watching her eagerly.* AD. *makes no sign of joy.* MAD. G. *gets off her knees, turns, offering both hands to child as she takes chair. Aloud.*] And you will never see me again.

Ad. Why not?

Mad. G. Because the Captain is going to take the lady and you far away. But if you ever have need of me, I will come to you. For you must know that I am your mother, [AD *exchanges looks with Ray.*] your second mother, or your third! In fact, I'm one of them, and that will do if you ever want me!

Ad. But you can write to me—I know how to read writing, and you can tell me where you are, and I promise to go to you right away if I should ever be a little orphan again—if I should lose my father and—and—

Mad. G. And—[*Watching her.*]

Ad. And—this lady! [AD. *runs to her mother, gets on her* R., *and embraces her.*]

Mad. G. [*Rises, aside.*] They are all deceiving me! But why? They shall betray themselves, though! [*Aloud.*] Well, I must be going. [*Rises and fusses with her hat, etc., aside.*] They don't try to keep me. [*Aloud.*] I have brought you some little presents, my dear. [*To Ad.*] They are in my carriage at the gate. Will you go and get them while I take leave of your parents. [AD. *runs out,* C.] There's a little darling! Run! [*Calling after her.*] Tell the coachman to give you the bundle! The horses won't move! They are gentle! There she goes! How she runs! [*Screams.*] Oh! good Heaven! [*Turns quickly to see the effect on* RAY., *who starts up in the greatest alarm.*]

Ray. [*Starting up.*] What is it?

Mad. G. [*Holding her back.*] She has fallen; she is covered with blood!

Ray. [*With a cry breaks away, and runs to the door.*] My child!

Mad. G. So then—[*catching her arm*] YOU are the mother! [*All stand transfixed.*] I was sure of it! Don't fret about the child. Nothing has happened to her. I did as you all have done! I told a falsehood. I was determined you should betray your secret!

Mon. Madame! [*Approaching her.* RAY. *sinks into chair.*]

Mad. G. [*To Mon., but going to Oct.*] Don't be afraid, I know what I'm about. [*To Oct.*] So you believed me to be altogether a fool, did you? I understand everything now! This child was yours, and you left her in the hands of mercenaries. This man was your friend, and to save yourself you made him take her as his own. And you stood by as the witness! You the father!! Coward! [*Moving from him.*]

Oct. [*Approaching her.*] It was for you.

Mad. G. It was for the money you expected to gain and to sport with, as you have sported with the feelings of these people. Where are the laws to punish such men as you? There are none! And this is what a man can do without a blush! No! I'm wrong. It is what *men* do!! [*Pointing to Mon.*] What a MAN does, HE does! Look at him! One that deserves the name! And to think I was about to marry you.

Oct. [*Approaching her.*] My dear—

Mad. G. It is over! You quit France or I do. Not a word! There's the door! Go!

Oct. [*Going* L., *pretending to weep.*] I go.

Mad. G. You had better.

Oct. May you be happy.

Mad. G. Oh, I am. Don't worry about me.

Oct. I am the victim of a plot. Between you, you have deprived me of the only creature I ever loved!

Going, meets ADRIENNE, L., *returning with her arms full of ribbons, parcels, laces, and a doll,—led by* JOVIN, *who carries a doll's cradle.* OCT. *going to embrace* AD., MAD. G. *pulls his arm, the child runs over to* RAY., *kneels beside her, showing her doll, and toys.*

Jovin. [*To Oct.*] You are to marry her—for her noble sake let us be friends. [*About to offer his hand.*]

Mad. G. [*Violently.*] Don't touch him! Come away from him. [JOV. *gets* L.]

Oct. Come now! I think you misapprehend the position in which this affair leaves me.

Mad. G. Bah! What do you mean?

Oct. It seems I have taken a deal of pains about other people's offspring, and here are my thanks. There stands the self-acknowledged father, and you are the self-acknowledged mother. If people wonder why I didn't marry you, why I do not visit this house, I point to the records of adoption! Could I wed a person who brazenly admits her own impropriety?— Never! Could I recognize a family that publishes its own shame? Never! The world is on my side! That is enough for me. I will have the sympathy and respect of society. I am obliged to you all for setting me up, and I wish you a very good evening! [*Exits,* c.]

Jov. Shall I follow, and take his affidavit?

Mad. G. [c.] Ah, well! So I've lost a husband I never had, and a child I couldn't get. [*To Ad., who goes over to her.*]

Mon. [*Holding his hand out to Ray.*] My wife!! [*Holding his other hand to Mad. G.*] My friend!!

Jov. [L.] Don't forget me!

Mad. G. Hush, I'll take care of you!

Ray. [*To Ad., embracing her.*] My darling!

Ad. [*Embracing Mon.*] Papa! [*Running to Mad. G., and hugging her.*] Mamma! [*Then to Ray., clasping her neck.*] Mother!

CURTAIN.